Sophie, in Shadow

Sophie, in Shadow

Eileen Kernaghan

thistledown press

Thistledown Press Ltd.
410 2nd Avenue North
Saskatoon, Saskatchewan, S7K 2C3
www.thistledownpress.com

Library and Archives Canada Cataloguing in Publication

Kernaghan, Eileen, author
Sophie, in shadow / Eileen Kernaghan.

Issued in print and electronic formats.
ISBN 978-1-927068-94-6 (pbk.).—ISBN 978-1-77187-016-0 (html)—-
ISBN 978-1-77187-017-7 (pdf)

I. Title.

PS8571.E695S66 2013   jC813'.54   C2014-900748-5
                             C2014-900749-3

Cover illustration detail by Amalia Chitulescu
Cover and book design by Jackie Forrie
Printed and bound in Canada

Canada Council Conseil des Arts   SASKATCHEWAN   Canadian   Patrimoine
for the Arts   du Canada   ARTS BOARD   Heritage   canadien

Thistledown Press gratefully acknowledges the financial assistance of the Canada
Council for the Arts, the Saskatchewan Arts Board, and the Government of Canada
through the Canada Book Fund for its publishing program.

*For my grandchildren
and in memory of my mother, Belinda Pritchard Monk*

Suppose time can slow down. Suppose it's not an ever rolling stream, but something altogether more viscous and unpredictable, like blood. Suppose it coagulates around terrible events, clots over them, stops the flow.
—Pat Barker, *Another World*

PROLOGUE

Darkness. The air frigid, the sea an infinite expanse of black glass. The sky glittering with stars. Somewhere music — a lively dance tune, ragtime — growing faint with distance as their lifeboat drifted away from the dying ship. The dark, the bitter cold, the sickening awareness of unthinkable loss. The ship's stern a monstrous finger pointing skyward, its ghostly lights still glimmering beneath the water. The music slow and sombre now, a familiar hymn. And then that terrible rising din of voices.

Sophie woke, shuddering and crying out. She sat up among the tumbled bedclothes, teeth chattering, throat clenched around a hard knot of terror and grief. The dream never changed. How many times was she doomed to relive in every detail the horror of that night?

Aunt Constance, in her nightdress, was already at her side.

"Aunt Constance, I'm so cold."

"I don't wonder, child. Look, you've thrown off all your covers." Aunt Constance closed the porthole against the night air, straightened the blankets and for good measure tucked a shawl around Sophie's shoulders. "Best wrap up before you catch your death."

But it was death caught me, *Aunt Constance.* The thought came, as Sophie's thoughts often did, unbidden. *He caught me, but then he let me go.*

Somewhere along the passageway a gramophone was playing. Some passengers returning late — from the second class lounge, Sophie supposed — were calling out goodnights.

She was warmer now. Presently the music died, doors clicked shut, and the passageway fell silent. Perhaps tonight, as they made their slow way eastward, there would be no more dreams of that earlier, ill-fated voyage.

ONE

1914

"You must expect to be disappointed," the other passengers told Sophie. Taking refuge in India was sensible now that Europe was at war, but nonetheless it was an experience to be suffered and endured. "The Taj Mahal by moonlight, pale hands beside the Shalimar — romantic balderdash," pronounced a bronzed and leathery colonel who was on his way back to the Frontier. India, everyone agreed, meant dirt and poverty, smothering heat, bad smells and indigestible food. "Not to mention revolting heathen practices," added the colonel's memsahib, declining to elaborate.

Of all this, Sophie was well aware. She had not much patience with romantic novels. She'd prepared for this journey, in her usual methodical way, by reading histories of the Raj and the Moghul Empire, and Himalayan travellers' tales. Though even those held out the promise of exotic splendours — minarets and gilded palaces, gardens in Kashmir.

In any event, whatever horrors awaited her in Calcutta, it would be a huge relief to disembark. Perhaps, out of reach of English newspapers, she would no longer be an object of such fascination. Just today she had come up on deck to overhear a snatch of conversation, hastily broken off.

"The poor lamb, to have lived through such an ordeal. To have both her parents drown when she was — how old? Fourteen? And now to be packed off to this godforsaken country, to live with relatives she's never met . . . " For two years now Sophie had been made to feel like public property — the survivor of a famous disaster, a name miraculously entered on the right side of a list, a curiosity to be interviewed and photographed and discussed. She yearned to be once again plain Sophie Pritchard, whose life was nobody's business but her own.

ℬ

"Merciful heavens, the heat!" said Aunt Constance, fanning her damp face with a dog-eared Cornhill Magazine. *She stood with Sophie on the steamer's foredeck as it made its way up the Hooghly past Garden Reach. "I fear it's bringing on a migraine. Will Delhi be cooler, do you think?" Even now, at the end of October, with the monsoon rains over and winter not far ahead, the air felt like a hot, wet blanket, thick with the swampy smell of the Ganges delta.*

"I expect it will," said Sophie, without much conviction. She and her aunt were soon to part company. Once Sophie had been safely delivered to her relatives, Aunt Constance would continue on to Delhi for a visit with her sister, who was married to a civil servant.

And as for these Calcutta relations — how little Sophie really knew about them! Tom Grenville-Smith was a zoologist, working at the Indian Museum. Jean, his wife, was an author — quite a successful one, Aunt Constance said.

Privately, Sophie hoped that her books were not the kind of popular romance that Aunt Constance preferred.

The river was crowded with every sort of craft — paddle steamers, big, solid square-sailed vessels and little fishing boats with upturned bows, barges and launches and bamboo rafts. Along the near bank were factories and warehouses, temples and walled riverside gardens, burning-ghats and derelict mansions, weed-covered skeletons of boats, and crowds of people standing knee-deep, waist-deep in the murky water of the bathing ghats, dressed in long robes, or loin-cloths, or nothing at all.

Now they were through the Floating Bridge, and here at last was Calcutta. India, Sophie suspected, was every bit as noisy, and chaotic, and bad-smelling, and bewildering as the colonel had described; but what mattered was that she would soon set foot on solid ground.

The wheel turns, and turns again. That, thought Sophie, is what Hindus believed. Her old life had ended on that disastrous April night in the North Atlantic. Now, for better or worse, as their ship ploughed its way up this swarming, clamorous Indian river, a new one was about to begin.

Two

JUST AS THEY WERE ABOUT to dock, Aunt Constance's migraine struck with full force. She had barely the strength to protest as Sophie helped her to bed.

"But Sophie, I must see you safely arrived . . . " Aunt Constance's voice was faint with pain.

"And so you have," said Sophie, as she drew the curtains against the light. "What you must do now is to rest. Someone is to meet me on the quay, and I'll be perfectly fine."

"But . . . " With a groan Aunt Constance fell back on her damp pillow. "You have the Delhi address? Promise you'll write the minute you're settled?"

"I promise," said Sophie as she leaned down to kiss her aunt's cheek.

"My brave girl!" sighed Aunt Constance.

If only that were true, thought Sophie. How she had dreaded this parting, from Aunt Constance and from all that remained of her old life. Yet there was impatience, too, in the midst of her sadness, to discover what might lie ahead.

ℊ∂

Encumbered by her cases, Sophie disembarked with the other Calcutta passengers into an immense confusion of noise and heat and jostling crowds.

Beggars, porters, street hawkers, goats, cows, baggage-laden travellers swarmed over the quayside. The air was thick with the acrid reeks of charcoal smoke and rotting vegetation. Queasy and disoriented, Sophie gazed round in despair. A determined looking Indian porter was pushing his way in her direction. But how much would he want to be paid, and could she trust him not to run off with her belongings? She shook her head, no.

Where in all this crush of humanity were the relatives who were meant to collect her?

Just then she caught sight of a tall Englishwoman who, from the vantage point of some nearby steps, was peering anxiously into the crowd. Sophie snatched off her hat and waved it frantically. The woman smiled, waved back, mouthed something Sophie could not make out. Then, closely followed by an Indian manservant, she forged her way towards Sophie.

Buoyed by the hope of rescue, Sophie called out "Mrs. Grenville-Smith?"

"Sophie! At last! I was afraid I'd somehow missed you. How was your voyage? Are you quite exhausted?"

"A little," said Sophie, wiping her damp forehead with her pocket handkerchief. In the clammy heat her long-sleeved shirtwaist was clinging to her skin, and her stays were pinching. She was beginning to feel quite faint. She envied Jean Grenville-Smith her loose-fitting tunic dress in teal-coloured silk, and sensible wide-brimmed straw hat.

"Good heavens," said Mrs. Grenville-Smith, "You look quite done in! We've brought the motorcar, and we'll get you home at once." Sophie stayed close behind her as she threaded her way through the crowd, the servant following with Sophie's cases.

Though freshly waxed and polished, the motorcar, a Ford four-seater, had dented fenders and looked as though it had seen hard use. The manservant took the wheel, expertly maneuvering his way around rickshaws, bicycles, bullock-carts and heedless pedestrians.

They drove past rows of palatial white buildings, splendidly domed, colonnaded, and porticoed, surrounded by trees and set in expanses of green lawn. *The City of Palaces*, thought Sophie, remembering Calcutta's old imperial name. None of it was quite what she had expected, and she started to say so — then paused, flustered.

"Oh dear, what shall I call you? Should I call you Aunt Jean?"

Jean Grenville-Smith laughed. "How elderly that sounds! What sort of relations are we, Sophie? Second cousins?"

"I'm Tom's first cousin once removed, I think," said Sophie, who had taken the trouble to look it up.

"Well, then. To Tom's cousins at whatever remove, I'm Jeannie."

Playing tour guide, Jeannie pointed out the sights as they turned from the Esplanade onto the Chowringhee Road. Here was the vast green parkland called the Maidan, with the high grey walls of Fort William beyond, more white palaces and villas, and the Indian Museum where Tom Grenville-Smith worked. Just ahead they could see towering cranes where construction of the Victoria Monument was in progress — "remarkably slow progress," remarked Jeannie. "One despairs of ever seeing it finished."

"And what is that?" asked Sophie, pointing to a slender column that rose from the Maidan, piercing the smoke-veiled upper air.

"That," said Jeannie," is a monument to Major-General Sir David Ochterlony, the conqueror of Nepal, who kept a harem of thirteen wives, and paraded them about on thirteen elephants. Or so the story goes. One day we'll climb the two hundred and eighteen steps, Sophie, and you can look out over the whole of Calcutta."

Presently they left the crowded thoroughfare of Chowringhee Road for Park Street, and came into an area of wide, quiet streets lined with cassia trees and solid mid-Victorian houses standing in their own walled gardens. Their driver turned into a side street, drove through wrought iron gates and drew up in the shady driveway of a tall veranda-encircled house, with white pillars guarding the entrance.

A stern looking manservant, turbanned and black bearded, greeted them at the door. Sophie, stepping into the cool interior and looking round, exclaimed, "What a marvelous house!" How different this was from Aunt Constance's cottage, with its dark mahogany furniture and faded carpets. They were standing in a long, high-ceilinged room with white-painted walls. Vivid Afghani carpets lay scattered over the marble floors. For furnishings there were some light bamboo chairs and settees piled with silk cushions, a carved rosewood cabinet, a few small brass-topped tables. Embroidered Indian hangings shared the walls with delicate botanical prints and drawings of exotic animals. It was just the sort of house where Sophie imagined a zoologist and an author would live—though in her experience, things seldom lived up so well to expectations. It was not home, any more than Aunt Constance's cottage had been home, but to Sophie it felt like a house where people could be happy.

"It *is* quite marvelous, isn't it?" Jeannie was saying. "And far too grand for this family. A few years ago when Calcutta was still the capital, we never could have afforded a house like this. It belonged to a government official, you see, and when they all decamped to Delhi, it was left standing empty, and so we seized the chance to lease it."

Their driver came in with Sophie's cases, and Jeannie broke off to say, "In the west bedroom, please, Thekong."

"The house is convenient, being close to the Museum," she went on, "but if it weren't for the small army of servants that came with the place, we should rattle around in it like three peas in a very large tea chest . . . Sophie, my dear, you must be exhausted. Let me show you to your bedroom, and then we'll have tea."

She led Sophie into a large, airy room with windows facing west. "We haven't done much in the way of decorating," she said, "as we thought you would like to choose your own things." Sophie could not imagine what else she might need, or want. There was a wood-framed bed with a bright Indian spread, a rosewood bureau and a comfortable chair, a large gilt-framed mirror, and on the floor a thick, soft rug in shades of red and purple and gold. A little Indian servant-girl was busy unpacking and putting away Sophie's clothes. Already, Sophie knew, they had begun to smell of Calcutta — that pungent mixture of smoke and vegetable decay.

After tea, served on the veranda by a waiter in impeccable whites, Sophie wandered out into the garden. This late in the year it was still ablaze with roses and crimson hibiscus. Bougainvillea clambered over a sundrenched wall. A girl of ten or eleven, clearly the daughter of the house, was sprawled on her stomach in the shade of a flowering tree, a book spread open in front of her.

"Hello," the girl said, glancing up at Sophie's approach. She was bare-legged, sandalled, wearing a faded cotton frock. "Are you Sophie?"

"I am."

The girl closed her book and sat up, pushing back a tangle of red-gold curls. "I'm Linnaea Alexandra Grenville-Smith."

"I'm very pleased to make your acquaintance," Sophie said.

"But for everyday I'm Alex, so if you prefer you can call me that." She gazed at Sophie with wide-set green eyes. She had a lively, intelligent face, generously daubed with freckles. Her expression was friendly enough, but all the same, Sophie felt that she was being discreetly judged.

"I believe I will," said Sophie. "It's easier to remember. But Linnaea Alexandra — what a pretty name."

"I know," said the child complacently. "It's Linnaea for Mr. Linnnaeus, who classified the plants and animals . . . "

"A fine name for a zoologist's daughter," Sophie agreed.

"And for a botanist too. That's what I plan to be, when I'm older. And Alexandra is for my mother's friend. My mother says I am a *petite sauvage*, just as Alexandra was at my age."

"And is that true?" asked Sophie. "Are you a wild child?"

"Not usually," said Alex, after a moment's consideration. "I believe the other Alexandra was a good deal wilder. She ran away from home when she was only five."

"Good gracious," said Sophie. "And where does she live, this other Alexandra?"

"I suppose, not anywhere in particular. Right now she is exploring the Himalayan Mountains."

Sophie, intrigued, made a mental note to ask Jeannie about this.

"My mother says you have come to live with us," said Alex.

"That seems to be the plan."

"Because of the war?"

Sophie nodded.

"That's why I'm here as well," said Alex. "I'm meant to be at school in England, which undoubtedly I would hate. My sister Diana's in England, learning to be a nurse, and she doesn't like it one bit. So I suppose in one way the war is a good thing."

"But surely not in any other way," said Sophie. "I can't imagine that war can ever be a good thing."

"I suppose not," conceded Alex. "I used to read those books by Mr. Henty — you know the ones, *With Clive in India*, *The Young Buglers* — and I imagined how splendid it must be to carry a sword and march in parades. But then I heard my mother say that she was glad she had only daughters, so she would not have to send her children off to war, for it was bad enough to have to send them away to England. So it was foolish of me, I suppose, to want to be a boy . . . "

"Yes," said Sophie. "Yes, I believe it was."

℘ə

Just before sundown Tom Grenville-Smith — a tall, soft-spoken man in vigorous middle age — arrived home from the museum. Dinner was served in the echoing vastness of the dining room. "There was a definite chill in the air this morning," said Jeannie, as they settled round the table. "We'll be needing a fire soon" — though Sophie, sweltering in her lightest cotton dress, found this difficult to imagine.

Aunt Constance's cook had sometimes produced what purported to be curry — chicken or lamb covered in a bland yellow sauce, with some nuts and raisins mixed in. It bore no resemblance to the exotically spiced dishes offered by the dignified manservant. Alex, now scrubbed and brushed and demure in her starched white frock, explained each dish to Sophie as it was served. There were vegetable-stuffed pastries — *samosas*, Alex said — as well as fish curry served with rice and accompanied by crisp puffs called *luchi*. Afterwards, instead of the sturdy pudding beloved of Aunt Constance's cook, there was fresh fruit — bananas, oranges, papayas, the last mangos of the season — and little coconut flavoured cakes called *pitha* ."We don't have those very often," said Alex, surreptitiously helping herself to another. "I asked cook to make them for you as a special treat."

"And what do you think of Calcutta so far?" Tom Grenville-Smith asked Sophie.

"I'm a little confused, "confessed Sophie. "I'm not sure what I was expecting . . . "

Tom laughed. "No doubt you've been reading Mr. Kipling's Calcutta sketches? 'The City of Dreadful Night' and so forth?"

Sophie nodded. It was one of many books she had brought to read on the ship.

"The smells and gross darkness of the night, in evil, time-rotten brickwork, and another wilderness of shut-up houses," said Tom, quoting. "But Kipling was not wrong. His Calcutta is as real as this one. There are not one but many Calcuttas, Sophie, as you'll discover."

ᔕᕒ

Much later, listening to the soft whir of the electric fan and the mysterious sounds of the Indian night, Sophie was exhausted but far too wrought up to sleep.

Nothing was quite as she had imagined it — from the noise and oppressive heat, the city's rank smells and crowded streets and lush unexpected gardens, to the calm and grace of this beautiful house. And the most agreeable surprise, thought Sophie, who had been prepared for the dullness of a settled middle-aged household — were these lively, youthful-seeming cousins.

Jean Grenville-Smith must be over forty now. Sophie had imagined her as another Aunt Constance — a solid, comfortable shape, imposing of bosom and broad of hip. But Jeanie's figure was slender still, her hair a vivid shade of reddish-gold, her green eyes lively. Aunt Constance had told Sophie something of Jeannie's history. She was the daughter of a Scottish schoolteacher, whose family, with the father's death, had fallen on hard times. "Once," said Aunt Constance, "hard as it is to imagine now, Jean worked in the fields as a common farm labourer."

Perhaps not entirely hard to imagine, thought Sophie, now that she had met Jeannie Grenville-Smith. There was a firmness of jaw, a plain-spokenness about her that in another woman might seem intimidating. She was a memsahib, after all, and that, Aunt Constance had emphasized, demanded dignity and presence. But when something particularly amused Jean Grenville-Smith — and more often than not it was one of Alex's sage pronouncements — her eyes danced, and she would turn away to hide a mischievous smile.

And Tom Grenville-Smith? Surely he must close on fifty — not bent and scholarly, as Sophie would have guessed, but tall and tanned and energetic. It was apparent to all that Jeannie and Tom doted on each other. When their eyes met, it was as though they shared some secret that the rest of the world was not to know.

. . . And then there was Alex . She was not quite sure what to make of Alex.

THREE

SOPHIE WOKE NEXT MORNING FROM a dreamless and unbroken sleep. In the confusion of first waking she could not think where she was. Somewhere nearby, two voices called out to each other in an unknown language. She could hear crows, the harsh cry of a peacock, the *scritch-scratch* of a broom sweeping gravel. When she sat up she saw mosquito netting draped over the bed, white walls surrounding her, a high white ceiling. Through the window came rich smells of flowers and wood smoke and spices. *Not Aunt Constance's dark English cottage; not the ship's cabin. I am here — I am truly in India.* And now the small, smiling Indian maid was tip-toeing to her bedside with a tray of tea and biscuits.

By the end of the first week Sophie was beginning to sort out Jeannie's "small army" — the bewildering number of servants that every self-respecting family was expected to employ. To save expense, Jeannie was managing without a butler. Nor did Alex have a governess — Jeannie had taken over her daughter's education, with regular lessons on weekday mornings. Instead there was the ayah, Lily, daughter of a Bengali mother and a British father. Lily, who had somewhat loosely defined duties as Alex's nurse and Jeannie's ladies' maid, was a rather flighty twenty year old with skin the colour of melted caramel and luminous dark eyes. She had been educated by nuns, and spoke perfect English with an oddly Irish lilt.

Mustapha, the bearded Moslem khitmutgar, a man of imposing height and presence, greeted visitors and waited table with fearsome dignity. The half-Portuguese cook, always addressed as Mr. D'Souza, produced Yorkshire pudding and mouth-searing fish curries with equal finesse. There were two Brahmin gardeners, high caste and aloof, and the little maid-of-all-work, who was called Lakshmi. And then there was Thekong, Tom's personal bearer, a Buddhist from the northern kingdom of Sikkim, a man of few words and imperturbable good humour. Alex clearly adored him. He was teaching her to shoot with a bow and arrows, and was always willing to join in games of hide and seek.

Those were the servants whose faces Sophie recognized, and whose names she could remember. There were besides, a sweeper, a general caretaker, a boy-of-all-work who helped the cook, a washerman and some part-time cleaners; and there, declared Jeannie, she had drawn the line.

"It terrified me at first," she confessed to Sophie. "I spent my girlhood taking orders, never thinking one day I must learn to give them. Still, one does what is needed, in order to get by."

There were survival skills, as well, that Sophie had to learn. "You must always watch out for poisonous snakes in the garden," Alex more than once reminded her. "And every morning you must check inside your boots for scorpions."

※

Alex had spread out a rug under a cassia tree and as usual on warm afternoons was reading a book. Today she was absorbed in a thick olive green volume with fanciful gilt decorations on the cover.

Sophie sank down beside her in the patch of shade, curling her legs beneath her. *"Peter and Wendy?* Is it good?"

"Oh yes," said Alex, "it's about some children in London whose ayah is a dog, and a boy called Peter teaches them to fly, and there are mermaids and pirates . . . I'm just getting to the pirates. I expect there will be battles too." She marked her page and politely set the book aside. "My mother is an author, you know."

"Yes," said Sophie. "My Aunt Constance told me."

On most afternoons Jeannie excused herself and vanished into a small sitting room on the shady side of the house, where Sophie guessed that she was working on another manuscript. According to Aunt Constance, Jean Guthrie had published several well-regarded novels, though no copies were to be found in Aunt Constance's village lending library. In any case, Aunt Constance, having read a review, felt the subject matter might be unsuitable for a girl of Sophie's age.

"They're not as exciting as this one," Alex said. "There are an awful lot of conversations and no battles at all."

"And no pirates?" asked Sophie.

"Exactly," Alex agreed, as she turned back to her page.

Unsuitable or not, Sophie had every intention of reading Jeannie Guthrie's books.

❧

In these cooler autumn days the family still breakfasted in the garden. The air was fresh, and filled with the scent of tropical flowers.

"Have some rumble-tumble," said Jeannie. "Scrambled eggs," explained Alex, giggling at Sophie's confusion. There was lentil *dhal* as well, with steaming heaps of rice, and as always a big basket of fresh fruit.

Sophie's thoughts drifted to other long-ago mornings, to breakfasts on the terrace in hazy Sussex autumns, when the air smelled of burning leaves. There would be kippers and kidneys and oatmeal, toast in the rack, and pots of ginger marmalade. She saw her mother pouring the tea, still slender and girlish as when she had been the Honourable Miss Sarah Montague. Her loosely knotted, flyaway hair was a pale gold nimbus that put Sophie in mind of dandelion floss. And there was her father, soberly dressed for Parliament, buttering a last piece of toast before he rushed off to catch the London train.

This was what Sophie's own life, surely, was meant to be: an uneventful passage into womanhood, courtship, marriage, marked by country weekends, hunt balls, London theatre parties . . . a safe, predictable existence from which she was suddenly wrenched by the incomprehensible workings of fate.

❦

Jeannie was looking through the morning's mail. "Aha," she said, plucking one from the pile. "Finally — a letter from Alexandra." She slit open the envelope and glanced over the first page. "It seems she has come down to Gangtok, long enough to communicate with the outside world."

"This is Jean's formidable friend Madame David-Neel," Tom told Sophie.

"Yes, Alex has been telling me about her. She sounds very adventurous . . . "

"Not to mention slightly mad," said Tom. "When last heard from, she was tramping about the Indian Himalayas, living on nettles and ferns, and trying to argue her way into Tibet."

Jean glanced through several closely written pages. "Nonetheless, it seems she has heard something of what is happening in the world. And she has a fair bit to say about it."

"I imagine she would," said Tom.

"She has had a letter from her husband in France. She says, 'Philip has written that we are at war. How proud I am, to know that our brave French soldiers have taken up arms in defense of civilization. If I were a man I would return at once to enlist.'"

"If she can't be a soldier, she could still be a nurse, like Diana," Alex pointed out.

"Alexandra as a nurse?" asked Tom. "In a starched cap, answering to the matron? I can't see it, somehow."

"Mr. Kipling wants everyone to do their part," said Alex.

Tom gave his daughter a quizzical look. "How would you know that?"

"It was in *The Statesman*," said Alex.

"Reading the newspaper, were you? Never a good plan," said her father. "It's been known to cause malignant vapours and swelling of the brain. Remind me to stop our subscription."

"Oh, don't tease the child, Tom," said Jeannie, laughing. "Pour me another cup of tea and I'll read you some more of this rather extraordinary letter."

"All of Alexandra's letters are extraordinary," said Tom. "Read on."

You may remember my telling you of the Gomchen of Lachen, whom I met while visiting my friend Prince Sidkeong in his palace at Gangtok. "Sidkeong is the Maharajah of Sikkim," Jean explained to Sophie. "Alexandra has been moving in exalted circles."

The Gomchen was at court to perform a tantric ceremony, and what a fascinating figure he was, in his five-sided crown, his necklace of skulls and apron of human bones, his hair in a long plait down to his feet, his eyes burning like hot coals.

"Oh, I should like to have seen that," said Alex.

"On the contrary," said her father. "You would have been frightened out of your wits."

"But let me continue," said Jean, turning to a new page. *The Gomchen is reputed to be a powerful sorcerer, who can fly, and command demons, and even kill people from very far off.*

"All useful skills," said Tom. "He should be recruited for the war effort."

"There's more," said Jean, laughing. "She goes on: *I have been visiting the Gomchen at his monastery overlooking the village of Lachen. My Tibetan has greatly improved during our long discussions on Buddhist teachings. One day at his invitation I climbed to his hermitage, The Cave of the Clear Light, twelve thousand feet in the sky. In that great solitude, surrounded by the eternal peaks, I felt immensely calm and at peace. It was then that I realized I had always been destined for the life of a hermit. If I prove worthy, I hope to study the secret teachings of tantric Buddhism.*

"Oh, dear," said Jean, putting down the letter. "How like Alexandra! She is caught up in another one of her enthusiasms."

"She tells the most wonderful stories," Alex told Sophie, reaching for another curry puff. "Do you know, she has been an opera singer, and a writer, and a world traveller, and an anarchist . . . "

"An anarchist?" said Sophie. "Really?"

"So it would seem, in her youth," Tom said. "I suspect that somewhere in Paris there is a police file with her name on it."

"Oh, Sophie, I do hope you can meet her," said Alex. She sent her mother an imploring look. "Do you suppose next summer when we go to the hills . . . ?"

"Clearly our Alexandra is a great admirer of her namesake," said Tom, "and seems bent on following in her footsteps."

FOUR

JUST AS SOPHIE, AT HOME in England, had counted the days
till Christmas, now Alex was counting the days to Diwali,
the Festival of Lights. With Diwali also came Durgapuja, the
Festival of Kali.

"Will you be taking Sophie to Kalighat to see the goddess?"
Alex asked.

Jeannie exchanged a quick glance with Tom. "I think
Sophie might find the experience too disturbing."

"Do you think you would be frightened of the goddess,
Sophie?" Without waiting for an answer, Alex declared, "I'm
not frightened, and I'm a lot younger than you."

"Perhaps not, "Jeannie said. "But then you've grown up in
Calcutta. You've seen plenty of Kali figures. Sophie might find
the goddess quite alarming."

"I'm not easily frightened," said Sophie. *Not any more.* And
as though she had heard that bleak thought spoken aloud,
Jeannie gave her a quick look of comprehension.

"She's all glittery black with a necklace of skulls round her
neck," said Alex, with obvious relish. "Her tongue is bright red
and so long it hangs out of her mouth, and she stands with one
foot on her husband's body, holding up a chopped-off head."

"Goodness," Sophie remarked, inadequately.

Alex, encouraged, went on, "And every night of Diwali she fights a great battle with the demon Asura, and all over the city there are lights burning, to help her win the fight."

"And why do you suppose she is sticking out her tongue?" inquired Sophie.

Smearing a generous portion of marmalade on her toast, Alex explained, "Most people think it's because she intends to drink somebody's blood. But the cook's boy says she's just embarrassed, because while she was rampaging about in fury, she accidentally stepped on her husband, the god Shiva. So it is as if she is saying, "Oh sorry, dear, please excuse me.""

Sophie laughed. "I like that explanation better! Though it can't be very pleasant for Shiva, being trod upon."

"Kali isn't only a goddess of death and destruction," Tom said. "Her worshippers would tell you that she represents time, change, empowerment . . . Seriously, Sophie, would it interest you to see the temple?"

"Since I'm to become a Calcuttan, I suppose I should learn as much about the city as I can."

"Quite right," said Tom. "Then I'll arrange an expedition."

ᏚᎦ

As they drove south along the Chowringhee towards Kalighat, past the interminably-under-construction Victoria Monument and Gothic spires of St. Paul's Cathedral, the grand buildings gave way to shops, hotels, and clubs. Here the stately Victorian mansions, now grown shabby, had been cut up into rooming houses.

The temple at Kalighat was surrounded by a crowded marketplace where dozens of stalls sold brass pots and kettles, picture postcards, clay images of the gods, brightly-coloured paintings on cheap paper, small goats clearly meant for sacrifice, and an intriguing array of cheap souvenirs. The air reeked of mustard oil and the swamp-smell from a nearby canal. Milling about among the stalls were travel-worn pilgrims, Brahmin gentlemen in pleated dhotis with their sari-clad ladies, saffron-robed devotees, naked longhaired sadhus.

The main roof of the temple was topped by a smaller roof and a pinnacle on top of that, with a raised platform all around. "We won't be allowed into the inner sanctum," said Tom, "even if we were prepared to spend hours in the line-up and risk being crushed to death by pilgrims. However, if we can find a spot on the platform with the rest of the tourists, we should still be able to see into the *sanctum sanctorum*."

They managed to find footholds in the press of onlookers gathered on the platform, all vying for a glimpse of the inner temple and the image of Kali Maa. Sophie maneuvered her way to the front, where there was a line of sight through the temple verandah to the inner sanctum. By craning her neck, it was just possible to see the area surrounding Kali's altar and Kali herself presiding over it.

This was not the painted image of the goddess that Sophie had seen everywhere throughout the city, nor did it resemble the clay figures sold in the marketplace. Neither was it the comic monster Alex had gleefully described. This Kali of black stone, with her long, grotesquely protruding golden tongue and her three huge glaring red eyes, must be, thought Sophie, the goddess at her darkest and most fearsome, the One Who Causes Madness. This was not an image of the deity in terrifying human form, but an image of terror itself, come down from the first days of the world.

Sophie could hear the chanting of the priests within the sanctum, the clash of cymbals in time to the mantra's hypnotic rhythm. In the space before the altar were heaps of marigolds and scarlet hibiscus, and a row of copper basins standing half in shadow.

Presently the temple musicians began to blow on conch shells and long curved trumpets.

Sophie drew in a horrified breath as the priests dragged before the altar a small, bleating goat smeared with vermilion powder. Another priest took hold of the animal, laid its head on the chopping block, and severed it with a single swift blow of the knife.

She wanted to look away, and found she could not. Standing amid closed-packed bodies in the heat of morning, she felt lightheaded, short of breath; her mouth was parched. The reek of the canal was mingled with the smell of incense, and human sweat, and rotting flowers. She thought she could drown in that thick air, unbreathable as swamp water. She felt herself swaying as her vision blurred; the world slipped sideways and her knees gave way.

Something had shifted, altered. She was standing ankle-deep in trampled flowers and blood-soaked mud. It was no longer morning, but the depths of night. The room flickered with torchlight. Great piles of goats' heads were heaped before the altar. There was blood everywhere. The air stank of death. The pulsing of the drums had risen to a fever pitch; her heart thudded to their insistent rhythm. Now she saw that the priests were scooping blood from copper basins and throwing it at Kali's feet.

Naked and cringing, a young boy was dragged forward, out of a long line of other young boys. And she saw that the heads before the altar were not, as she had first imagined, the heads of goats.

৯৯

"Sophie!" Dimly she heard Jeannie's voice, crying out in distress. With no notion of how she got there, Sophie found herself sitting on some steps with her head resting on her knees.

"Just keep your head down, Sophie." That was Tom's reassuring voice. "You'll be all right in a moment. You've fainted, that's all."

And Jeannie, sounding frightened and contrite: "Poor lass, it was too much for her. It's too soon; it's the wrong place for her to be."

But where had she been? Not here on this sunlit platform, in the midst of a noisy, excited crowd. For a few strange moments she had stood alone at midnight in a place where she could not possibly be. Wrenched out of time, she had stood before Kali's blood-drenched altar, trembling with awe and terror under that pitiless gaze.

๛

At night the whole of Calcutta was alight, with candles burning on rooftops and verandas, clay lamps on every windowsill. Fireworks streaked across the sky, exploding in showers of golden fire.

"Do you think," said Alex, "if I climbed to a mountain top, like Alexandra, I could look down and see all of India lit up with Diwali lights?"

"Perhaps you could," said Sophie, "if you climbed high enough."

She wanted to share Alex's enjoyment of the incandescent night; and yet a twinkling line of lights along a parapet, the brilliant skyward path of a rocket, the sound of voices calling out in darkness could suddenly make her mouth go dry, her throat constrict.

What had happened to her in the Kali temple? A waking dream? A hallucination brought on by too much heat and excitement?

She had hoped when she stepped from the river steamer onto the Calcutta wharf that she was leaving the nightmares behind. But however it happened, that brief vision of horror in Kali's temple had shattered the fragile balance she had fought for two years to achieve. She thought with sudden anger, *Is this how the rest of my life is to be? When every flare of light in the night, every voice in the dark, reminds me not of celebration, but of death?*

Five

THE NOVEMBER MORNING WAS PLEASANTLY cool, with a thin fog just starting to lift. *An English morning,* thought Sophie, remembering the burst of energy that used to come with the first days of autumn, when holidays were over and a new school year was beginning. But that part of her life was over. If she was not to become as bored and languid as the Calcutta memsahibs of other centuries, she must find some useful way to fill her days. Like those earlier expatriate Englishwomen, she could wander about the countryside with easel and watercolours, seeking the "picturesque", or she could write long obsessively detailed letters home. But letters to whom? Aunt Constance was off having her own adventures in Delhi.

Still wearing her dressing gown, Sophie wandered out onto the veranda. She found Jeannie, looking as though she had been up for hours, setting out pansies in large stone pots.

"There," said Jeannie, smoothing the soil around the plants with a practised hand. "My little bit of England." She took off her gardening gloves, and pushed back a stray lock of hair. "Now then, Sophie. I'm off on a mission in search of a book. I thought you might like to come along."

Books! Sophie knew she would soon exhaust the possibilities of Tom's and Jeannie's personal libraries, which seemed mostly to consist of zoological treatises and atlases of India. ("We left most of our books in England," Jeannie had explained. "The summers here are ruinous to paper and cloth.")

"It's one that Tom has managed to misplace," said Jeannie — "Professor Lydekker's *The Wild Animals of India, Burma, Malaya and Tibet.* Probably abandoned in some Himalayan rest-house, halfway up a mountainside. But it's an important work, and I'd like to buy him a new copy as a birthday gift — so if we find one, Sophie, you are sworn to silence."

Thekong, who usually drove, was at the museum with Tom, so it was Jeannie who took the wheel of the Ford. After a few hesitant coughs the vehicle started obligingly enough, though once underway, as Sophie nervously observed, it produced an ominous cloud of black exhaust.

"I know," sighed Jeannie. "Poor thing, it's suffered frightful abuse on these Indian roads. Ready for the boneyard soon, Tom says. Though somehow Thekong always manages to keep it going."

From the wide, straight thoroughfare of Lower Circular Road they turned into a neighborhood of narrow curving streets, lined by tall shabby buildings that shut out all but a sliver of the sky. Jeannie calmly steered the automobile through a maze of twisting, potholed lanes jammed with rickshaws, bullock carts and wandering cows. Pedestrians, crowded off the pavements by food stands, tea stalls, hawkers' makeshift booths, spilled into the middle of the road. As a rickshaw-wallah pelted past with his load of crates, Sophie decided that would be a more sensible way to travel these streets than in a balky motorcar.

College Street, Jeannie had said, was in the university area, surrounded by schools and colleges— hence its name — and was the centre of Calcutta's intellectual life. Sophie had expected to find a street of dignified antiquarian bookshops, like the ones in Charing Cross Road. On visits to London she had loved those shops with their smells of old leather, old paper and dust — the rare volumes lovingly preserved behind glass and cheaper ones stacked in odd corners.

What she found, instead, when they turned into College Street, was a crowded roadside path lined with dozens of small open air bookstalls. When Jeannie had managed to shoe-horn the Ford into an empty space and paid a boy to mind it, they joined the throng of browsers searching through haphazard piles of second-hand volumes. All jumbled together were well-thumbed popular novels, university texts, Greek philosophy, cheap editions of Jane Austen and the classics, valuable looking antique books bound in leather and gilt. While Jeannie proceeded methodically from one stall to the next in search of the Lydekker, Sophie unearthed a copy of Mr. Kipling's *Kim* to re-read in its native setting, and the letters in two volumes of the Hon. Miss Emily Eden, sister of an earlier Governor-General, who had lived in Calcutta at the height of her Imperial glory some seventy-five years before. She added a copy of *Mansfield Park*, which she had yet to read, and as for Alex's botanical library, a book of Indian plants with coloured plates.

"Oh my word," she heard Jeannie remark. She glanced up to see Jeannie holding out a small paperbound volume. "Imagine that! Here's Alexandra's anarchist tract. I wonder how it made its way here from Paris?"

Sophie thumbed through the book. The print was small, and in French. "*Pour la vie,* by Alexandra Myrial?"

"Yes, that's our Alexandra," said Jeannie. "She was wise enough to use a *nom de plume.* I'd better buy it," she added. "If it should fall into the wrong hands the British will have more reason than ever to keep a close eye on Alexandra. I believe they already have her police dossier from those Paris days."

"Alexandra, an anarchist?" said Sophie, handing back the book. Though she remembered Tom saying something of the sort.

"Oh indeed, an anarchist — or a would-be one, at any rate."

Jeannie paid for the book and put it away in her bag. They followed the leafy path round College Square, which was occupied by one of the vast pools of water the Indians called a tank. Still more book racks were set up along the railings of the college buildings, but these seemed to be mostly old examination papers and tattered paperbacks.

Jeannie was walking more quickly, almost purposefully now. Sophie lagged a little behind, still keeping an eye out for literary treasures. She looked up to see that Jeannie had paused on the steps of the Sanskrit College, in the company of a tall, middle-aged Englishman, who, though not in uniform, had a distinctly military look. He was a type familiar to Sophie from shipboard — clipped moustache, soldierly bearing, face tanned and leathery from long exposure to the Indian sun. She was not close enough to overhear their conversation, but glancing discreetly over a portfolio of faded watercolours, she saw him slip something — a letter, a piece of paper, a pamphlet? — into Jeannie's hand. Quickly, without looking down, Jeannie tucked the paper it into her jacket pocket.

Then, with a brief formal nod to Jeannie, the man turned and walked away,

Was I not meant to see that? The oddness of the encounter aroused Sophie's curiosity, as well as a vague unease. She caught up to Jeannie, who said casually, "An acquaintance of Tom's, on leave from the Frontier. I should have introduced you, but I'm embarrassed to say I've utterly forgot his name." She said nothing about the paper in her pocket. It was as though that surreptitious exchange had never taken place.

"Did you find Tom's book?" Sophie asked, as they returned to the auto.

"I'm afraid not," Jeannie said. "But I've asked one or two booksellers to keep an eye out for me. Straight home, then?"

Sophie nodded. The day had turned hot and humid, and her energy was flagging. What she wanted now was shade, and rest, and an hour or so of solitude. Something she did not understand had occurred just now in College Square — something that she knew would trouble her as long as it was unexplained. Could it have been an assignation . . . a tryst? Such things happened in Anglo-India, she knew — but she could not bear to imagine it of Jeannie. There had been no hint of intimacy in that brief meeting. And in any case, why invite Sophie along as an observer? By the time they drew up at the house Sophie had rejected the whole notion as absurd.

Still, some sort of rendezvous had clearly taken place. Only later did it occur to Sophie why she had been invited along. In the close-knit, gossipy expat community, Jeannie would not wish to be seen driving alone to College Square in order to meet a man who was not her husband — however innocent the reason.

Six

THERE WAS MIST IN THE evenings now, and an early morning chill. English flowers — roses, sweet peas, chrysanthemums — flourished in the garden. Alex was in dire need of new winter clothes, and so on a day of clear skies and crisp yellow sunshine Jeannie proposed an expedition in search of dress material. In Dalhousie Square, where grand imperial buildings surrounded a man-made lake, Alex stopped to read the inscription on an obelisk.

"Look, Sophie, that's where they put those people into the Black Hole."

"Alex!" Jeannie said sharply. "That's such a dreadful story. I don't think Sophie needs to be reminded of it."

"But it's history," Alex protested. "Sophie, do you know about the Black Hole?"

Of course Sophie knew. Surely every school child in England knew what happened when the Nawab of Bengal invaded Calcutta with fifty thousand soldiers and four hundred battle elephants, and they came with ladders to storm Fort William. One hundred and forty-six people, soldiers and civilians alike, crushed together in a tiny room in the suffocating heat of the Calcutta summer, with no water, no air, not an inch of space to sit or lie down. The prisoners climbed on trampled bodies as they tried to catch a breath of air from the high barred windows. And in the morning one hundred and twenty-three were dead, mostly where they stood. *As though they had drowned in air.* Sophie felt her throat tightening, the familiar sick lurching of her stomach. She thrust the thought away.

Perhaps it was all a hoax, as many people nowadays said. Perhaps there had been far fewer people (for how could so many be crammed into so small a space?) or perhaps it had not happened at all, but was one of those myths that grow out of war, for all that the true stories are terrible enough.

"That's a piece of history best forgotten," Jeannie said, "It may not give you bad dreams, Alex, but I can't speak for Sophie. Best head back to the car now — we still have to order you those winter shoes."

The shoemaker had his shop in a lane off Chitpur Road. This was a Muslim district, and the shops were full of treasures — Mughal perfume in cut glass jars, caps embroidered in gold and silver thread, musical instruments, and Islamic medicines, heaps of nuts and dates and pomegranates.

Once Alex had been fitted for her shoes they stopped at a sweet shop to buy some of the syrupy white sweets called rosogollas that were Alex's favourite treat. Jeannie was handing over some coins to the shopkeeper when Thekong, who had been waiting with the motor car, suddenly appeared in the open doorway.

"Memsahibs, stay inside — there is trouble!"

At that moment Sophie heard what sounded like gunfire — then shouts, and running feet, and a babble of excited voices.

Thekong had seized Alex's hand and was pulling her away from the counter into a far corner of the shop. Bewildered,

Sophie turned to look out into the street, but a crowd had gathered, blocking her view of whatever was taking place. Then Jeannie grasped her firmly by the arm and drew her back from the doorway.

"What's happening . . . " Sophie tried to ask, but Jeannie shook her head, a finger to her lips.

Presently Thekong went to peer out. "Safe now," he said. "Memsahibs, best I am taking you home."

Outside, the crowd was already dispersing. A rickshaw sat abandoned in the middle of the street. Under its wheels was a spreading pool of blood.

"Alex, don't hang about — and don't stare. Just get into the car — now!" Sophie could hear the shrill note of urgency in Jeannie's voice.

Once back on the Chowringhee Road, Sophie broke the silence. "Jeannie, please, can you tell me what happened?"

Jeannie hesitated. "I think it was most likely a *dacoity* — an armed robbery."

"Armed robbers? Here?"

"Indeed yes, robbers. Don't look so alarmed, Sophie. I believe we were safe enough. They rarely attack English people — at least, not here, in public. But for the well-off Indians, it's always a danger, especially since the start of the war."

"Perhaps," put in Alex, "it wasn't a *dacoity*, it was an assassination." And Jeannie quelled her with a stern look.

Later, as she sat reading on a bench in the garden, Sophie heard Jeannie's voice, then Tom's. They had come out to walk on the veranda in the cool night air, and seemed unaware of Sophie's presence.

Tom — as though echoing Alex's earlier words — said, "It wasn't a *dacoity*, was it? In broad daylight, in the middle of the street?"

And Jeannie, answering: "No. Anyway, not the usual sort. Thekong says the attackers looked like students."

"Revolutionaries, then. And the man who was shot?"

"A wealthy Hindu businessman, apparently. Another attempt to raise money for the cause."

Sophie, listening, felt her world abruptly shift. Surely terrorism and revolution belonged to places like Russia, or to history books? Though the shadow of war lay over Europe, she had imagined that this sheltered enclave of imperial Britain, with its grey fortress walls and tall white houses, its well-ordered world of band concerts, cricket matches, luncheons at the club, would somehow remain untouched. But suddenly there was gunfire in the streets, blood on the pavement, and children who spoke far too matter-of-factly of assassination.

"Not a bomb this time, thank God," she heard Tom say. "But they're getting bolder."

Sophie closed her book and went inside, for the dark was gathering, and the night seemed suddenly full of unsuspected terrors.

※

Sophie woke long after midnight, crying out as she so often did, in terror and despair. It was not, this time, the endlessly revisited dream of death by water, but a confused and feverish vision of fire and blood.

"Sophie, my dear, what is it?" It took Sophie a moment to realize that was Jeannie's voice, not Aunt Constance's. She sat up, and things came slowly into focus.

Jeannie sat down on the edge of the bed and drew aside the netting to feel Sophie's forehead.

"Another nightmare?" she asked, pushing back a damp tendril of Sophie's hair.

Sophie nodded.

The little housemaid had appeared in the doorway, looking frightened and concerned. "Lakshmi," said Jeannie, "will you fetch me a wet cloth?" And in moment or two the girl returned with a small towel and a bowl of water.

Pressing the cool towel to Sophie's temples, Jeannie said softly, "You know, I've wondered how wise it was, to bring you here."

"To India? But . . . "

"Oh, Sophie, I don't mean we don't want you, we do with all our hearts. It's lovely for us, and for Alex, to have you here. But for someone who has so narrowly escaped death, who watched death claim the people she loves . . . Sophie, I'm not sure what it is I'm trying to say."

"I think I know," said Sophie. "The Kali temple, and yesterday, the blood in the street . . . "

" . . . was more than you could bear. Yes. At first it was for me, as well. India is so crowded with ghosts, death such an inescapable presence. But I learned to look past the darkness, and see that there is also beauty here, and grace, and splendour. Alex has seen that from the beginning. Perhaps in time you will as well."

And then that other Jeannie, the take-charge, unflappable Memsahib Grenville-Smith, said as briskly as Aunt Constance might have done, "So. The Museum tomorrow, then?"

"Yes, please," said Sophie, feeling oddly comforted, and lay back on her damp pillow, hoping for sleep.

SEVEN

THE INDIAN MUSEUM WHERE TOM worked was a vast white Victorian edifice, part Italian Renaissance, part ancient Greek. From the arcaded courtyard Jeannie, Sophie, and Alex stepped through tall doors into a cavernous interior. "Zoology to the left, art to the right," said Jeannie. Staircases rising from either side of the entrance hall led to the upper galleries, which, cautioned Jeannie, were not quite as grand as the majestic exterior would lead one to expect. "A bit dank and badly lit, I'm afraid. Tom complains that there is never enough money for upkeep. But before we go upstairs, Sophie, I want you to see the Buddhist antiquities," and she led them through the entrance hall past slender pillars topped with bull and lion capitals, into a long, high-ceilinged gallery filled with carvings of the life of Buddha.

"They're nearly two thousand years old," said Alex, relishing the role of museum guide as they admired the fanciful menagerie of monkeys and elephants, lions and cobras accompanying the Buddha on his journey to enlightenment. Presently she asked her mother, "May I visit the elephants?"

"You may," said Jeannie, and smiled as her daughter politely excused herself and hurried off. "She's gone to see the giant prehistoric elephants across the hall," Jeannie explained.

"Or their skeletons, at any rate. They fascinate her. What an odd child I seem to have raised!"

Jeannie and Sophie went on to a second room filled with holy figures sculpted in stone — graceful almond-eyed boddhisatvas from the ancient civilization of Gandhara. *Beauty and grace and splendour*, thought Sophie. In the serenely smiling presence of these images from a vanished world, she felt a lightness of spirit she had not experienced for a very long time.

৪৯

Tom's office was upstairs in one of the Zoological Galleries. Jeannie led the way along a corridor lined with slightly dusty specimen cases to a closed door marked "Deputy Superintendent, Natural History Section." She knocked, and after a moment Tom called out, "Come in." As they entered, he was folding up a map or chart that had been spread out across his desk. "Jeanie, Alex, look who's just turned up," he said, and a tall red-haired man standing beside the desk gave them an engaging grin. Though he was in civilian dress, his stiffly waxed ginger moustache lent him, thought Sophie, a distinctly military air.

"Major Bradley," said Jeannie. "We heard you were in France. How splendid to have you back!"

"Sophie," said Tom, "may I introduce my old friend James Bradley? In another life, we were undergraduates together at Cambridge — and James, this is Miss Sophie Pritchard, a young relative of ours from England."

"Delighted, Miss Pritchard," said the major, offering Sophie his hand. "You're here for a holiday, then?"

Sophie felt herself blushing. How should she explain her situation? She did not wish to be thought one of those young

Englishwomen who came to India for no reason but to find a husband. She was grateful when Jeannie came to the rescue: "Sophie is here for an extended visit, Major. And I see that you're in mufti — have you left the army, then?"

"For the time being," said Bradley. He cast a wry glance at the walking stick in his left hand. "I took a bullet in the leg at the Marne. No great matter, and it's healing nicely, but they've seen fit to put me on leave."

"You fought in France?" asked Alex, clearly awestruck.

"That I did, young Alex. With the British Expeditionary Force. Very damp and foggy, France."

"Alex has been following the progress of the war," said Tom.

"Best not," said the major, a trifle brusquely. "In any event, I'm headed north in a day or two — some business needs my attention in Sikkim. All very hush-hush" he added, giving Alex a conspiratorial grin.

"Alexandra is in Sikkim," said Alex. "Living in a cave."

"Is she indeed? The formidable Madame David-Neel? And is she as mad as ever?"

"So it would seem," Tom said.

"Then I must certainly look her up. I have the greatest admiration for that woman. She's the only memsahib I know who speaks Tibetan better than I do myself."

Eight

TOM HAD *THE TIMES OF INDIA* spread out across the breakfast table. "Here's a distressing piece of news," he said. "The Maharajah of Sikkim is dead."

"Oh dear!" said Jeannie, paling a little. "Does it say how it happened? Wasn't he quite young?"

"Thirty-five," said Tom, handing over the paper. "And no, it doesn't say. I expect someone at the museum will have the inside story."

Jeannie folded the *Times* at the obituary page and read aloud:

We regretfully announce the death on December 4 of his Highness Sidkeong Tulku, Maharajah of Sikkim, at the age of 35 years. The Maharajah Kumar Sidkeong Tulku of Sikkim was the son and heir of the late Sir Theotub Mangyal, and succeeded his father as ruler of Sikkim in February of this year.

The Maharajah Sidkeong was a fine linguist, being conversant in English, Hindi, Nepali, Lepcha, Tibetan, and the Chinese languages. He was a Director in charge of Ecclesiastical, Forest, and Education Departments of Sikkim, and was an Honorary Lieutenant of the Northern Bengal Mounted Rifles in 1913. His home was at Gangtok, Sikkim, and he was a member of the Darjeeling Gymkhana. He was unmarried.

"What a dreadful waste," said Jeannie, putting down the paper and turning to Sophie. "Alexandra will be distraught. She and the Maharajah were such great friends."

ℰ

Lachen, 17 December

Ma chère Jeanne,
Je suis desolé. I have had the most dreadful news. I have just learned of the sudden death of my dear young friend Sidkeong, the Maharajah of Sikkim, under strange and inexplicable circumstances.

Tom set down the piece of toast he had just buttered. "Strange and inexplicable circumstances?"

"Wait, let me go on," said Jeannie, scanning the rest of the letter. "I see that she drops dark hints."

Officially he is said to have contracted jaundice, which brought on a heart attack, but I am not willing to accept this explanation. He was too young and strong, too full of health and vigour. How many happy hours have I spent wandering through the mountains with him as my guide and tutor. On our last foray into the mountains I was hard put to keep up with him as he leaped like an antelope from rock to rock. When we parted on that day — I to continue my upward journey towards Tibet, he to return to his royal duties — he waved to me with his Swiss mountaineer's hat, calling out to me "Safe journey!" Little did I imagine that we would never meet again.

I am bereft of a treasured friend. My only comfort is that he was said to be a tulku, a reincarnate lama, who was able to choose the date of his death, to be reborn at some more auspicious time. But Jeanne, why would he choose to die now, at the height of his youthful powers, with a glorious career ahead of him?

There is a rumour among the monks that with his modern ways he offended his ancestral spirits. But I have my own suspicions that we should look instead to his stepmother Queen Drolma. He described her to me once as a woman of utter ruthlessness, and his greatest enemy.

Or perhaps the British have had a hand in this. They have found Sidkeong too wise and too strong-minded a ruler to be a mere puppet of the British throne.

Whatever the facts — and indeed, they may never be known — I am inconsolable. But this unhappy circumstance has brought me to a decision. I plan to spend the winter here in Lachen and return in the spring to the Cave of Clear Light, for I wish to learn as much as I can from the Gomchen of Lachen. He is known as a man of immense wisdom and mystical knowledge, a sorcerer if you wish.

How transient, how ephemeral is our time on earth, Jeanne. Only the mountains are everlasting and imperishable.

Alexandra

ॐ

Jeannie put down the letter with a sigh.

"Trust Alexandra to blame the British," Tom observed.

"You can understand why," said Jeannie a little tartly. "They refused her permission to visit Bhutan. She'll not soon forgive them for that. And when she applied through the

French ambassador to study in Tibet, they interfered with that as well."

"I believe," said Tom, "It was the Maharajah of Bhutan who refused permission. Alexandra does have a reputation for being meddlesome. And as for Tibet — there's a worry in certain quarters that she may be a spy."

This was addressed to Sophie, who was listening, fascinated. The more she heard about Alexandra, the more she seemed like a character in a book by Mr. Kipling.

"Best burn that letter," Tom said, and Sophie realized that he was in deadly earnest.

ℱ

Sophie woke before daylight from a restless sleep. It was in early mornings like this, before the rest of the family was awake, that she found herself turning over in her mind the events of the previous day. There was so much in this seemingly ordinary household that she did not understand — things overheard or hinted at, things unexplained.

Her thoughts wandered to the mysterious Alexandra. Could she and the young Maharajah have been more than friends? That thought was too sad to bear thinking about. Worse still, could there be any truth in Alexandra's suspicions? How terrible to think of the young Maharajah's life so suddenly snuffed out. Death, it seemed, was lurking everywhere, waiting to pounce on those who least expected and least deserved it.

NINE

EARLY IN DECEMBER, JEAN AND Sophie drove to the New Market to stock up on candied peel, nuts and sultanas for the Christmas cakes and puddings. Alex stuffed rupees into the gooey centres of the cakes before Mr. D'Souza wrapped them in greaseproof paper and put them away to ripen for Christmas Day.

Nearby Park Street twinkled the whole of its length with fairy lights. On gift-buying expeditions Alex stopped at every shop and restaurant window to admire the decorations. Then as the holiday approached delivery wallahs arrived at the door with mysterious packages from the Army & Navy Stores or Whiteaway & Laidlaw. There were poinsettias on the chimney-piece and carol singers at the door. Sophie, who was clever with figures, had been helping with Alex's lessons; but now the schoolbooks were closed until the new year. Instead, Sophie was enlisted to wrap Indian sweets in bits of coloured foil to decorate the tree.

On Christmas morning, after an early service at St. Paul's Cathedral, Sophie and Alex helped distribute gifts to the servants — Alex wearing her new red velvet frock and handing out the packages with a great sense of occasion. The servants in turn presented the family with baskets of flowers and sweets, and then came a big Christmas lunch with roasted duck.

The time-honoured traditions of Sophie's childhood — the morning walk to church, the servants' gift-giving, the Christmas bird, the sweets and crackers and paper hats — all were faithfully preserved in this faraway place, and yet nothing was quite the same. When Sophie opened Aunt Constance's greeting card with its scene of the snow-covered English countryside, her throat tightened with sudden homesickness. She remembered sleigh rides, and walking with her mother through the winter fields, carrying yuletide hampers for their tenants. She remembered watching from an upstairs landing, hours past her bedtime, as dancers swirled in silk and velvet across the ballroom floor. She remembered the giant spruce that at home in England had grazed the drawing room ceiling and glittered with hundreds of delicate glass balls. But surely now with the war those idyllic English Christmases would, like so much else, have vanished into memory.

In the afternoon, there was wine and rose cookies for friends who dropped by (Lily keeping a close watch on Alex for fear she would make herself ill). The friends who came round were for the most part Tom's museum colleagues and their wives, along with some English acquaintances in Calcutta for the holidays. With her fellow memsahibs Jeannie seemed on cordial but not especially intimate terms. They smiled and nodded on the street, but rarely exchanged visits. Sophie found the Park Street memsahibs with their genteel accents, their modish gowns and air of unquestioned privilege altogether too intimidating. She suspected that Jeannie felt the same.

၄ာ

After Christmas, there were cool, misty mornings and days of rain that kept everyone indoors — like an English autumn, thought Sophie with a pang of nostalgia — though here it was not the fragrance of burning leaves that hung in the air, but dung smoke.

With the end of winter came Holi, the Hindu festival of colours. Holi was a day of utter abandon, with processions all over the city, music and dancing and exuberant throwing of coloured powder on passersby. The servants, who had been out celebrating all day, returned in the evening stained with garish powder from head to foot — only to have Alex, laughing, spray them all with coloured water.

Then it was spring and everywhere the trees burst into pink, scarlet, orange, gold, and purple blossom. "It's such a beautiful day," said Jeannie one Saturday as Sophie was finishing her breakfast. "Tom's gone to work, Lily is taking Alex to visit her sister. We have the morning to ourselves. While it's still cool I thought you might like to do some exploring."

Sophie had not realized how many of the leafy open spaces nearby were burial grounds. Inside the wrought iron gate of the Park Street Cemetery they followed a path between rows of obelisks, urns, pagodas, cenotaphs — elaborate monuments to centuries of British dead. In spite of the bright spring sunshine, Sophie found it a gloomy place. That sense of oppression deepened as they read the names and dates engraved on the tombs. The bones of so many young men and women, so many children, rested here. She paused by a stone angel who sheltered three smiling stone cherubs with her outstretched wings.

Mary Bingham, beloved wife of Richard Bingham
died July 16, 1782 aged 32 years
Theodore Bingham d. July 18 1782 aged 10 years
Anne Bingham d. July 15 1782 aged 5 years
Elizabeth Bingham d. July 4, 1782 aged 5 months

"How terrible," Sophie said. "The mother and three children, all dead in a fortnight."

"It was all too common in those times," said Jeannie. "Most likely it was malaria, or cholera. They called it the pucka fever, but whatever it was, it was a dreadful disease that could kill in a day."

They moved on down the path. "And here's the grave of the famous Rose Aylmer,' said Jeannie, pausing by a small tomb topped by a cone-shaped pillar. "Dead at twenty, 'of a surfeit of pineapples'. That makes Alex laugh, but she shouldn't, because it's a tragic story. Just one of so many tragic stories."

Sophie read aloud from the poem inscribed on the plaque: "*What was her fate? Long, long before her hour, death called her tender soul . . .* "

"Rose Aylmer is famous because she had a poem written about her," Jeannie said. "But there were so many other young women who came out from England to marry, who simply faded away and died before their life had a chance to begin."

Sophie, only half listening, was beginning to feel oddly lightheaded. The sun had grown hotter; the air seemed stifling. The avenue of tombs seemed to close in upon her, forming a narrow passageway through which she moved without volition. She sensed a shifting, a dislocation, a diminishing of the light as though a cloud had passed across the sun. She thought, confusedly, *this has happened before.*

There was a sharp medicinal odour, and underlying it, a sour smell of sickness. The curtains were closed, the room in semi-darkness. A child lay in a cradle, its eyes closed, its limbs flaccid, its small pinched face a sickly yellow. A woman in a night robe bent over the cradle. Her long dark hair was matted with sweat, her damp face the same sallow colour as the child's. Overhead a huge wooden fan swayed to and fro, barely stirring the heavy air.

And then as suddenly Sophie was back in the cemetery, shielding her eyes against the dazzle of light.

"Sophie, my dear, what's wrong?" Jeannie was looking at her with concern and faint alarm. "You've gone as pale as a ghost."

Sophie's legs felt shaky; she wanted badly to sit down. "It's nothing," she said. "I just went a little giddy, that's all."

"A bit more than a little," said Jeannie. "For a moment you looked as though you were somewhere else entirely."

"I was," Sophie said. She knew it was hopeless to try to explain, but Jeannie was gazing at her so intently she knew she must make the attempt. "Jeannie, I know you won't believe me, but for one moment everything went dark, it was the middle of the night and the cemetery had vanished." Now that she had begun, there was no turning back. "I didn't know where I was, just that I was in a strange room where there was a woman, and a child who was dreadfully ill — I think it was dying. An instant, that's all, and then it was gone. But I was there."

She waited for Jeannie to say that it must have been a moment of disorientation, a trick of the light, a waking dream . . . She knew it was none of those things. She had seen the punkah coolie squatting in a corner, drawing on a rope to work the fan. She had seen the pictures on the walls — water-colour English landscapes, gilt-framed family portraits. She had seen the chintz cushioned rocking chair, the flowered cambric curtains, the embroidered coverlet on the baby's cradle. She had heard the slow creak of the wooden fan, the mother's laboured breathing as she bent over the cradle. The sickroom smell was still in her throat. Surely if that anguished mother had looked up for an instant, she would have glimpsed Sophie standing in the shadows by the door.

Jeannie drew Sophie to a nearby bench and sat down beside her. She waited until Sophie looked up and met her gaze. "Sophie, "she said, "Has this happened before? Is this what happened in the Kali temple?"

Sophie remembered torchlight, rotting flowers, blood-soaked mud. Her stomach churned.

"Yes," she said.

"Sophie, promise you won't speak of this to anyone else."

"I won't. Of course I won't. People would think I'd gone mad."

"Indeed they might," said Jeannie, with a hint of a smile. "People do go mad, in India. But Sophie, if you say it happened, then I believe you."

"But how can you possibly . . . "

" . . . believe you? Because I know there are things in this world that can't be easily explained. Because things have happened in my life, too, that I don't speak of, for fear of being thought mad."

"What things . . . " Sophie started to ask, but Jeannie waved away the question. "To come as close to death as you have — it can't help but leave a mark. You'll never be quite the same person you once were. Stronger, perhaps — but not the same. Sometimes you'll see things other people can't. That doesn't make you mad. Far from it."

Jeannie stood up, brushed dust from the back of her skirt, held out a hand to Sophie.

"All the same, I can see how much this is troubling you, and it troubles me as well. Would you mind very much if I wrote to Alexandra? She has a way of making sense of the inexplicable. And," she added, "Alexandra is the last person in the world to think you mad."

TEN

"THIS CAME TODAY," SAID JEANNIE, and she held out to Sophie a stained and travel-distressed brown paper envelope. "Rerouted through Kabul, from the look of it. Alexandra is writing to me, but I thought you would want to see it."

Gangtok, Sikkim

Ma chère Jeanne,
I have received at last your letter of last month and I make haste to reply.

In India, the veils between the worlds are thin. There are great rewards for those who would explore the mysteries that lie beyond ordinary experience. But for someone like your Sophie those veils may be especially fragile. For her, India may prove to be a dangerous place.

Ma chère amie, you understand this all too well, I think. Are you not reminded, as am I, of another jeune fille who long ago stepped through those veils and found herself in peril?

I would never suggest that your Sophie should not experience the riches of mind and spirit this country

*offers. I only say to you, chère Jeanne, that you should
recall the dangers.*

*I will be at the monastery above Lachen for much
of the summer, as I prepare for the winter that I plan
to spend in my hermit's cave. When you come north I
hope you will be able to visit me there — the climb is a
steep one, but the arrival well worth every effort.*
*I look forward to meeting Sophie, and will advise her in
any way that I can.*

Alexandra

Sophie glanced up from the letter.

"I know," said Jeannie. "It's not very reassuring. is it? But
one is careful these days what one puts in letters. I'm sure
Alexandra will have a good deal more to say when you meet
her."

Sophie felt as much puzzled as alarmed by the letter.
Who was the *jeune fille* who had found herself in peril? Was
Alexandra speaking of herself?

But Jeannie, clearly anticipating the question, seemed
unwilling to explain.

ELEVEN

B Y MID-APRIL THE HEAT WAS making everyone ill-tempered and lethargic. Sophie, sleeping under a thin sheet to the steady whirr of the ceiling fan, woke to find both sheet and nightdress soaked through with sweat. No wonder, she thought, that the ladies of the Raj in earlier centuries had succumbed to migraines, melancholia, fainting spells, and lassitude. Following Jeannie's sensible example, she had abandoned her stays and had taken to wearing simple, loose-fitting tunic-dresses.

"But don't pack away your cool-weather things," warned Jeannie. "You'll need them in the hills." Like most English families in Calcutta, the Grenville-Smiths were to spend the summer months at the hill-station of Darjeeling, and finally came the long-anticipated morning of departure. Piles of luggage and bedding were assembled on the verandas, tiffin-baskets were packed with buttered buns and hard-boiled eggs, bottles filled with boiled water and lemonade. The servants who would stay behind were given last-minute instructions, and in the grey light of early morning the family, along with Thekong and Alex's ayah Lily, made their way to the railway station. Tom, who had work to finish at the museum, was to follow in May.

The platform was crowded with poor Indian families who had been camped there all night waiting for their trains. Goats and chickens — and the occasional sacred cow — wandered among the cooking pots and piles of bedding. Jeannie had insisted that Lily must travel with the family in their second-class compartment, but no such consideration was possible for Thekong.

"Third class is horrid," observed Alex, as they settled themselves on the padded leather seats which at night would be made up into narrow bunks. "I wish Thekong could stay with us."

"I wish he could too," said Jeannie. "But I'm afraid I must be a proper memsahib and you must be a proper memsahib's daughter, and abide by the rules."

"For fear of drawing attention to ourselves," said Alex.

Jeannie gave her a quick, surprised look. "Where did you hear that, Alex? Did someone tell you that?"

"Oh, it was a long time ago," said Alex. "When I was quite little. I was at the zoo with Lily . . . wasn't I, Lily? — and I tripped and scraped my knee, and I cried — quite loudly, I expect — and a lady said "Hush, child, you're drawing attention to yourself.""

"Yes, well," said Jeannie. "That's usually good advice."

"Alexandra draws attention to herself," Alex remarked. "And she would have let her friend the Maharajah ride in the carriage with her."

"Alexandra doesn't feel a need to abide by the rules," replied Jeannie, smiling. "Any more than do Maharajahs. It's different for ordinary mortals."

"It's especially different if you're an Indian," said Sophie, thinking unhappily of Thekong. Already, on this first morning of their overnight journey, Sophie was breathless and exhausted. The sun beating down on the metal roof of the train turned their compartment into an inferno. She could only imagine what travel must be like for the Indian passengers, tightly packed into the third class carriages, with no space to lie down, nowhere to sit but on their luggage or the floor.

"It's what I like least about India," Jeannie said. "There are so many divisions — not just of race, but of caste and wealth and class. You cross those barriers at your own risk. Diana writes that things are changing in England, especially since the start of the war — but here we're still living in the past, in Queen Victoria's time."

Sophie was reminded, suddenly, that when Jeannie still lived in Scotland, before she married Tom, she had worked on a farm as a common labourer. That too had been in Queen Victoria's time. How much more aware must Jeannie be of those divisions, than someone like Sophie, raised in wealth and privilege.

As the day wore on, Sophie grew tired of gazing out the window at the sunbaked plain. There was little to see but scattered villages set among dried-up rice and jute and mustard fields. Alex and Lily had both fallen asleep, with Alex's head in Lily's lap. Presently Sophie too slipped into a doze.

Some time later, she woke as brakes shrilled and the train slowed to a halt. She looked out the open window and saw that they were at a station. There was a great bustle and commotion going on. Children stood between the tracks and reached up to the train windows to beg for coins; hawkers ran along the platform with trays of fruit and sweets, cheap jewelry and painted wooden toys, or bottles of garishly coloured drinks.

Alex sat up, looking dazed and a little feverish. Her face was sheened with perspiration. "I'm thirsty," she complained, and Jeannie dug into one of the baskets on the floor for a bottle of water. Just then a fruit seller went by the window, carrying a tray of bananas on his head.

"And hungry," added Alex. "Could we buy some fruit?"

Jeannie glanced over at Lily, still sound asleep and gently snoring. "I'll go," she said. "There's a news-seller too — Sophie, I'll get us some magazines." She stood up, straightened her crumpled skirt, put on her straw hat, and stepped out of the compartment onto the platform, locking the door behind her.

Moments later, from farther down the platform, there were angry shouts. Someone—a woman — shrieked. There were more shouts — in Bengali, Sophie guessed. Then came the sudden crack of rifle fire.

Sophie froze in her place, her heart racing, her stomach twisting into a knot. Without stopping to think, scarcely realizing what she was saying, she cried out, "Alex, Lily — get under the seats."

Alex and Lily stared at her, eyes wide with alarm.

"Now!" said Sophie. Her voice was trembling, but still it carried an authority she hadn't known she possessed.

Lucknow, Cawnpore, the mutiny — women and children kidnapped, chopped to pieces, thrown down wells . . . Those terrible stories flashed through her mind. *Lock the door,* she thought. *No, the door is locked. Shut the windows, close the shutters.*

And as Alex and Lily, bewildered but obedient, scrambled for cover, Sophie reached towards the nearest window, slammed it shut and pulled down the louvred wooden blinds.

Before she had time to deal with the other windows, something thrust itself through the bars and shutters on the side of the carriage facing the tracks. It was a long, thin pole with a hook on the end.

It seemed to Sophie, even in her panic, that it was an odd sort of weapon, but the hook looked sharp and dangerous, and she had charges to protect. She seized the middle part of the pole in both hands, carefully avoiding the hook, and braced against the edge of a seat, she began to force it back through the bars. On the other side of the window, someone grunted. Sophie pushed again, hard, and there was no more resistance. She heard the thud of the pole as it fell onto the tracks, and the sound of feet hitting the ground.

But now someone was hammering on the door of the compartment.

"Sophie, open up, let me in!" Jeannie's voice. Sophie unlocked the door, and Jeannie stepped in, carrying a bunch of bananas in one hand, and some copies of the *Strand* in the other,

Limp with relief, Sophie sank down on the bench. Her throat had gone tight and raw, and tears were spilling down her cheeks. Meanwhile, Lily and Alex, hearing Jeannie's voice, had emerged rumpled and dust-covered from beneath the seats.

"Sophie, whatever is the matter?" Jeannie handed the bananas to Lily, tossed aside the magazines and sat down beside Sophie, holding out a clean handkerchief.

"I heard shots," Sophie gasped out between sobs. "Then a pole with a hook on it came through the window . . . "

"Oh Sophie, my dear, I'm so sorry, you must have been terrified . . . "

"I heard shots . . . " Sophie repeated helplessly.

"Yes, I know, some thieves were trying to steal bags from the platform. A soldier fired over their heads to frighten them off."

"But the pole, the hook . . . "

"Oh dear, I didn't think to warn you — that's a favourite thief's trick. They climb up and reach through the windows into the compartments. The idea is to catch up a bag or a parcel and drag out it through the bars."

"I thought . . . " began Sophie, but stumbled into silence. What, after all, had she thought?

"And you told Alex and Lily to hide?"

"I'm sorry, I . . . "

"Sophie, don't be sorry, I'm proud of you — you did exactly the right thing. "

Lily had dampened her handkerchief from a water bottle, and was wiping Alex's dirt-smeared face.

"We thought they were thuggee," declared Alex. "And Sophie was very brave, wasn't she, Lily? She frightened them off."

Twelve

"THUGGEE?" SAID SOPHIE. "You mean robbers, cutthroats?"

"Stranglers," declared Alex, with a certain amount of relish. Clearly, she had more to say on the subject, but Jeannie gave her the sort of discouraging look that Sophie's Nanny Perkins had once used to quell a talkative Sophie.

"Really, Alex," said Jeannie. "Sophie's just had a great fright, Lily as well. Must we talk about thuggee?"

"But it's . . . " Alex started to protest.

"Oh, yes, I know, it is history." Jeannie said. "Or at any rate, some version of it. Thuggee did exist — still does, I expect," she told Sophie, "but really, it's all become the stuff of penny dreadfuls."

Sophie was secretly rather fond of penny dreadfuls, and she guessed that Alex was as well. Besides, the journey ahead promised to be long and tedious. "I've read about the thugs," she said, "and really, I'd like to know more if Alex wants to tell me."

That was enough encouragement for Alex. "What they do, you see, is to make friends with travellers, and offer them things to eat and drink, but the food and drink is drugged, and then when the victims fall asleep, the thugs strangle them.

With a silver cord. Or sometimes if they haven't brought their silver cord, they might just use their handkerchief."

"But why would they do that?" asked Sophie. "So they can rob the travellers?"

"I dare say they do that as well," said Alex. "But mostly it's because thugs worship Kali, and she is a very fierce goddess, always demanding sacrifices."

Kali again, thought Sophie, suppressing a shudder.

"Oh, and I have to tell you about jaggeree. That's a kind of sugar which is sacred to Kali, and if you eat it then you are bound forever to the goddess. So you must be very careful when you travel not to eat jaggeree."

"Or you could become one of the thuggee yourself?"

"You might," agreed Alex, looking grave at the prospect.

"Alex," asked Jeannie in mock despair, "wherever do you hear these stories?"

"From Mr. D'Souza's son, Diego. He has a book about the thugs. He won't let me borrow it though because he says I'm a girl and I would be too frightened by the pictures."

"I think," sighed Jeannie, "that I had better have a word with Mr. D'Souza."

Thirteen

Early next morning they woke to find that they had come to the very foot of the Himalayas. The air was cool and pleasant after the heat of the plains. Above the grey haze of the plains, beyond foothills hidden in early mist, rose line upon line of purple mountains, and towering above all were the three shining white peaks of the sacred mountain Kanchenjunga.

Now, announced Alex, came the best part of the journey. They had an early breakfast in the Siliguri station restaurant, and then it was time to board the little train that would carry them into the mountains on its steep circuitous track The Darjeeling-Himalayan railway, with its spinach-green engine and bulging coal bunkers, its miniature compartments, was for all the world like a toy train in a children's book. From their first-class carriage, Sophie could look back and see the third-class passengers perched precariously on window ledges, chattering with their neighbours as they smoked their leaf-wrapped Indian cigarettes. Then the whistle sounded. Steam hissed from the tall funnel, and with a sudden jerk of the engine they were on their way.

Their journey began through dense green walls of jungle; then, as they began their ascent, they climbed past stands of giant bamboo and forests of huge trees canopied with liana vines and hung with orchid blooms. They crept past tea plantations clinging to narrow mountain terraces and hillsides vivid with scarlet and yellow and purple rhododendron.

All that day the little engine crisscrossed and looped and zigzagged its way uphill, hugging rock walls or creeping stolidly along the edge of an abyss. At times the track was so steep that a coolie standing on a ledge in front of the engine had to sprinkle sand on the rails so that the wheels could grip. The strong, sweet, burnt-leaf smell of Indian cigarettes drifting from the third-class carriage mingled with steam billowing from the engine, and, as they climbed higher, with thick white mist.

Sophie gazed out, entranced. She revelled in the coolness of the mountain air, the brilliant green of the foliage with its paint-box splashes of colour; the breath-stopping glimpses down sheer precipices to the plains below. Most of all, she delighted in the wonderful oddity of this journey. Fearful of heights, she should have been nervous as they skirted the edges of cliffs where the ground plunged sheer away into shadowy chasms. Strangely, she was not. Their doll's engine clung sturdily to its narrow rails; their track seemed safely anchored to solid rock.

"Do you like to imagine things, Sophie?" Like all of Alex's questions, it was a serious one.

"I did when I was your age," replied Sophie.

"Not now?"

"Sometimes." But when, thought Sophie, was the last time she had dared to let herself imagine anything?

"When we go to Darjeeling," said Alex, "I pretend our train is carrying us up into the sky, to a magic cloud kingdom."

Sophie laughed. "Then we'll imagine that together, and who knows — between the two of us, we might make it come true."

They passed through a thick bank of fog and there for a moment was a dazzling sunlit view of Mount Kanchenjunga; then more tea gardens, and at last, mist-shrouded, came Ghoom — the highest railway station in the world, read Alex from the guidebook she had bought at Siliguri station. Finally, in fading light, they made the short looping, roundabout descent into Darjeeling.

Fourteen

"THINK OF DARJEELING AS A seaside holiday, without the sea," said Jeannie; and Sophie, remembering childhood excursions to Bognor Regis, felt at once a familiar atmosphere about the town.

Jeannie had booked a proper house for the season, not just a cottage or bungalow. It was sparsely furnished and a bit rundown, but there was space enough for Sophie to have her own bedroom, while Lily and Alex shared another larger one. Thekong, who had made himself a comfortable space in an outbuilding, was now man-of-all-work, and Jeannie had hired a woman from the town to clean and cook.

"A far cry," said Jeannie, as she surveyed their Spartan drawing room, "from the days when the memsahibs arrived with twelve camel loads of household goods, including the grand piano!"

The house, like all Darjeeling houses, stood on a hill, and was surrounded by an unkempt rose garden. There were tea gardens on the slopes beyond and the snow capped mountains rising behind. On the Mall — one of the few flat places besides the parade ground — there were shops, cafés, an English library and a proper theatre where visiting players performed. The grey spires of English churches rose among minarets and temple towers. Early mornings were filled with the mists of remembered English autumns, and the night sky was brilliant with stars.

For Sophie and Alex, and for Lily as well, arriving in the hills was like recovering from a long fever. The lassitude of the plains was forgotten; they were filled with projects and enthusiasms. In this gloriously cool mountain air there were picnics to be organized, shops and bazaars to be explored, adventures to be sought out. One morning, waking from another long and dreamless sleep, Sophie realized that she was almost entirely happy.

Jeannie, meanwhile, spent much of her time on the veranda with her pen and notebook. She was working on her next novel, said Alex, with an air of having privileged information. Sophie had taken a surreptitious peek inside the book when Jeannie, suddenly called away to a kitchen emergency, left it lying on the table. Curiously enough, what she saw in that quick glance did not look at all like a manuscript page. Rather it was a long series of lists of what appeared to be Indian place names, with dates beside them. They must be research notes for the novel, Sophie decided, and closed the cover guiltily when she heard approaching footsteps. Jeannie, returning from the kitchen, gave the notebook an anxious look and quickly put it away.

છ૱

Major Bradley, on leave from Sikkim, came to lunch. Alex was eager for news of the war, but the major, looking unusually somber, seemed reluctant to discuss what was happening in Europe. Instead, Jeanie turned the conversation to the always intriguing subject of Alexandra David-Neel and her Himalayan exploits. "Did you visit Alexandra in Sikkim?" she asked the major.

"Indeed, yes. I clambered up to her mountain hermitage. Wouldn't have missed it for the world."

"And she is well?" asked Jeannie.

"I found her so. I think she is still recovering from the loss of her friend the Maharajah. She seems sad when she talks about him. All the same, I must say she looks quite fit and healthy."

"We plan to visit her in a few weeks' time," said Jeannie, pouring the tea.

"That will cheer her up no end," the major said. "And Miss Pritchard, I know she is most anxious to meet you."

"Sophie says she's never a met a hermit," Alex observed.

"Has she not?" said Major Bradley, turning to Sophie. "Well, Miss Pritchard . . . " Under his interested gaze Sophie felt herself blush. "You'll find that Madame David-Neel is not your ordinary run of hermit. Still, you should get on well enough with her. Just mind you take a stout pair of walking boots, and take care not get caught up in any of her mad schemes."

After lunch, Sophie and Lily took Alex off to explore the Indian bazaar. Alex had seen a necklace of Tibetan silver and turquoise she planned to buy for Lily's birthday. As they left, Jeannie and Major Bradley were sitting companionably on the veranda. Glancing back, Sophie noticed Jeannie leaning forward to show the major something written in her notebook. How odd, thought Sophie, considering that those pages were so zealously hidden from casual eyes. Perhaps Jeannie was asking the major to check her research. That made sense — though there was still a niggling doubt in Sophie's mind.

Surely there could be no romantic attachment between Jeannie and Major Bradley. And if there were, would they not take greater pains to conceal it? The same uncomfortable question had crossed Sophie's mind that day in College Street, when Jeannie had slipped a message — for surely it was a message — into her pocket, thinking she was unobserved. But then, as now, Sophie had thrust the thought away. Jeannie was a woman of honour. No one could have been more obvious in her love for Tom and her steadfast loyalty to him. But more and more in this pleasant, welcoming household, there were hints of things she did not understand and questions she sensed it was wiser not to ask.

Fifteen

For the journey to Sikkim Jeannie had packed their hired motorcar with warm clothes and blankets, packets of sandwiches and bottles of lemonade, along with some fruit conserves and other treats for Alexandra David-Neel, who had mentioned how weary she had become of lentils and beans. (*How I long for the taste of fresh asparagus*, one of her letters had lamented.)

As well, Jeannie and Sophie had each brought a silk dinner gown, along with Alex's best muslin frock. They would be staying in Gangtok as guests of Sir Charles Bell, the British Political Officer in Sikkim, who, Jeannie said, kept a very conventional household where they would be expected to dress for dinner.

The road from Darjeeling to Gangtok, following the valley of the River Teesta, wound for most of a day through a hazy landscape of oak trees hung with ferns and orchids, and wrapped in trailing mosses. Steep banks fell away to the river, and snow-capped mountains loomed beyond.

From time to time Sophie's stomach rose into her chest as they swerved and jounced and rattled their way along the rutted track, but Thekong, Sikkimese born, assured them that at this time of year, neither they nor the motorcar would come to any great harm. "Not like monsoon season," he told them. "Monsoon season, whole road washes away."

Jeannie and Thekong rode in a companionable silence; Alex, thrilled at the prospect of seeing her namesake again, took advantage of her captive audience and entertained Sophie with Alexandra stories.

"Imagine, Sophie! When she was only seventeen she hiked across the Alps all by herself and her mother had to fetch her back from Italy."

"I'm very glad," said Jeannie from the front seat, "that I was not Alexandra's mother."

"And when she came to India," continued Alex, "she hid behind a statue in the temple of the fish-eyed goddess and watched the secret tantric rites — I'm not sure what those are, she wouldn't tell me, but it is forbidden for anyone to see them . . . "

"Alex, hush!" Jeannie, sounding horrified, interrupted her daughter in mid-sentence. "Wherever did you hear that?"

"Why, from Alexandra, of course."

"Oh dear," said Jeannie. And turning round to Sophie: "Alexandra may be my oldest and dearest friend, but I do wonder sometimes about her common sense."

৯৯

Gangtok, the Sikkimese capital, clung to a hillside, surrounded by terraced rice fields. It was a city of Buddhist shrines and temples, fluttering prayer flags, brightly painted pagoda-shaped wooden houses built on flower-covered slopes. Rising in the distance were the snowy Himalayan peaks, and to the west, towering above all, the sacred mountain Kachenjunga.

The British Residency was an imposing white villa built in the English style with gables and bay windows. It stood in wide lawns at one end of a ridge overlooking the town. Sir Charles Bell, who welcomed them at the front door, was a tall, fair-haired, studious looking gentleman, a little humourless on first impression. He seemed to Sophie more like an Oxford don than a civil servant, and Jeannie had mentioned that he was a Tibetan scholar.

Jeannie and Sophie dined on their first evening with Sir Charles and his wife, Lady Cashie Bell. For Alex there was a light English supper with Lily, and early bed.

Lady Bell was a stately woman with a gracious if somewhat imperious manner, who seemed born to the memsahib's role. Dinner in the dark wainscoted dining room with its solid English furniture was a formal affair, with crystal glassware, Crown Derby china, monogrammed silver, and a silent host of white-clad servants. As the mulligatawny soup was brought round, Sir Charles Bell remarked to Jeannie, "We've quite enjoyed the company of your friend Madame David-Neel. She's a fascinating woman, and very knowledgeable about Buddhism. It's a philosophy in which I myself am deeply interested, and of which I hope to make a serious study once I retire. So we had much in common, and some very entertaining conversations."

Jeannie said, "Alexandra has been a devoted student of Buddhism, and all things oriental, as long as I've known her."

"Indeed, yes. She speaks Tibetan as well as I do myself."

"Hence," remarked Lady Bell, "the entertaining conversations. Much of the time I had not the slightest idea what was being said."

"However . . . " and here Sir Charles set down his soup spoon and cleared his throat. "If I may be quite frank, Mrs. Grenville-Smith . . . "

Jeannie smiled demurely. The look in her eyes told Sophie she knew well enough what was coming next.

" . . . I will say this, that you would be doing a service to the British Government if you could persuade Madame David-Neel to accompany you when you return to Calcutta."

"I suspect," said Jeannie, "that she has been making a nuisance of herself."

"Oh, I would not have put it quite as strongly as that. As I say, she is a charming and intelligent woman, for whom I have the greatest respect. But when she first arrived here, she was dead set on visiting Bhutan — and as you know, permission to travel in Bhutan is very rarely granted. She asked me to speak on her behalf to the Maharajah of Bhutan when I met him in Simla at the Anglo-Chinese-Tibetan conference. In fact, I did speak to the Maharajah — though she refuses to believe me. It was the Maharajah himself who declined to have her blundering about the Bhutanese monasteries — and probably opening the way for a flock of Christian missionaries to follow in her wake. And then, far from being discouraged, she applied through the French Ambassador's office for admission to Tibet."

With a sigh he reached for his wineglass. "You're aware, I'm sure, that because of an agreement with the Russian government, private travellers are not permitted to enter Tibet without Russia's consent."

"It has always been Alexandra's dream to visit Lhasa," Jeannie murmured.

"And mine as well," said Sir Charles, with a touch of acerbity. "While the Dalai Lama was in exile in Darjeeling, we became good friends, and now that he is restored to power, he has several times invited me to visit him in Lhasa. To my great disappointment, even I am not allowed to accept. Madame

David-Neel should realize that in the present situation, what with war in Europe and the Chinese only recently expelled from Lhasa, such expeditions as she proposes are out of the question."

Russia. Tibet. Expeditions to Lhasa. Sophie, tired after the day's journey and trying not to doze over her plate, began to listen more closely. How much like a page from *Kim* this sounded — how like Mr. Kipling's stories of the Great Game. But surely that belonged to an earlier time?

"Madame David Neel is not easily discouraged," remarked Lady Bell. "I think it has something to do with being French. She is relentless in pursuit of these . . . " she hesitated, seeking a word.

"Enthusiasms?" suggested Jeannie.

"Enthusiasms. Exactly," said Sir Charles. "And I have to say, that with all I have on my plate at present, I find her enthusiasms a little exhausting."

Sixteen

AN INVITATION ARRIVED AT THE British Residency inviting the Bells and their visitors to tea at the palace — which was in fact a large bungalow built in the British style with a red-painted iron roof and verandas around the sides. It stood, a little lower than the Residency, at the other end of the flowery promenade they called The Ridge.

The Dowager Queen Drolma received them in a sitting room filled with overstuffed chintz-covered sofas pushed against the walls, and a great many small tables scattered about. The walls were covered in a rose-patterned English paper, and tea arrived in a silver pot, on a tray with flowered china teacups and tiny silver spoons.

Queen Drolma was a small, slender woman, still handsome though no longer young: a regal figure in crimson silk and a dazzling amount of heavy gold jewelry. What Sophie noticed, more than the gorgeousness of her robes and the rich weight of gold at throat and ears and wrists, was the coldness in her dark eyes, the hard set of her mouth. She looked, thought Sophie, as though she had agreed to perform a tedious duty and would much prefer to be somewhere else. She did not seem to speak any English and responded to their polite small talk — translated by Charles Bell into Sikkimese — with a terse phrase or two, or simply a nod. When Lady Bell remarked on how fond they had all been of Prince Sidkeong, and how distressed by his death, the Dowager Queen's response was a faint, somewhat absent-minded smile. She seemed, thought Sophie, remarkably unaffected by her stepson's fate.

The tea party went on for a long time, with Jeannie and the Bells doing their best to keep up the one-sided conversation, while the servants refilled the teacups as fast as they were emptied. Though Alex was trying hard to play the part of a well-behaved young English lady, she was starting to fidget. At the moment she was tugging absently on one of her ringlets while her gaze drifted through the window into the sunny garden.

"Sophie," said Lady Bell, "perhaps you could take Alexandra for a walk in the palace gardens. That is if Her Highness has no objection?"

Charles inquired, and Her Highness nodded without much interest. Presently a young female servant was summoned to escort Sophie and Alex outdoors.

As they followed the girl along a corridor, Alex whispered, "Doesn't Queen Drolma make you think of the Red Queen in *Alice*?"

"She does, a bit," said Sophie, smiling.

"I was afraid," said Alex, "that she was going to say 'Off with their heads!'"

Part way along the passage they came to a door that stood slightly ajar — left unlatched perhaps by a careless servant. Alex, with her usual curiosity, stopped to open it wider and peer inside. The room was filled with sunlight, and through a window on the far wall they glimpsed a view of the mountains. Elsewhere in the palace, as far as Sophie had seen, the rooms were quite dark and often windowless. She wondered why this large bright space had dustcovers over the furniture and was apparently unused.

Unused — and yet not empty. Standing with Alex in the doorway while the servant waited in dutiful silence, Sophie felt a premonitory chill. There was a presence in this room, unseen but palpable — a vague dark thickening of the air, a gathering of shadow in a sunlit place where no shadow should exist.

And then without warning something clutched at her chest so that it was hard to breathe. There was a harsh, acrid burning in her throat and lungs, a sensation of stifling heat and a weight crushing down on her. Her head throbbed, her stomach churned with a sudden nausea. Dizzy and disoriented, she felt herself swaying, her knees threatening to give way. The servant reached out just in time to steady her with a hand beneath her elbow.

With an immense effort, Sophie drew herself upright. She stepped back from the doorsill, moved down the hall, and quickly as it had happened, it was over. Her head cleared, her breath came more easily, her stomach settled. The strength returned to her limbs. She looked round and saw the servant was staring at her in dismay. *She thinks she will be blamed for this,* Sophie thought; and she smiled, a little shakily, to show that nothing was amiss.

Whatever horror had once happened in that room, Sophie knew she had come perilously close to witnessing it. The ineradicable presence of death, the enduring resonance of it, was like dark water seeping through the fabric of time; now it was threatening to engulf her.

Seventeen

O N A CLEAR SPRING MORNING, Jeannie, Sophie, and Alex, with Thekong as their guide and protector, set out on the long anticipated journey to Alexandra's hermitage.

For the fifty mile trek up the forested mountain track to Lachen, Thekong had hired four surefooted Sikkimese horses, with a pack mule to carry their provisions. Growing up in the English countryside Sophie had been a capable horsewoman. She found that the old skills quickly returned. At night, grateful for a fire and hot food, they slept in a *dak* bungalow built along the way for the convenience of travellers.

Lachen, the last village before the northern border of Sikkim and the high passes of Tibet, was little more than a cluster of yak-herders' huts, perched on a hillside ablaze with rhododendrons. Nearby was a Protestant mission, and further up on another slope a small monastery where Alexandra's friend the famous Gomchen kept an apartment. To visit Alexandra in her hermit's cave they must climb still higher, almost to the Tibetan frontier.

Even at this height the branches of the trees were covered with orchid blooms, and Alex pointed out the rare species she recognized from her botanical texts.

From the flowering woods they came out into a clearing at the foot of a bare and desolate mountainside. Further up under a ridge of black rock they could see the fluttering prayer flags of Alexandra's hermitage.

It did not occur to Sophie at first that the small, stoutish, round-faced woman in the drab monk's robe who came down the steep path to meet them could be Alexandra. This was surely not the wild and willful, daring heroine of Sophie's imagination. But Alexandra it was indeed, and she clasped Jeannie in her arms with a cry of delight.

"Chère Jeanne! At last! And Alex — *mignonne! Très jolie,* and so tall! And here is Mademoiselle Pritchard! You must come up to my cave at once, and I will order tea."

৪৯

Sophie's notion of a hermit's cave was a cold, dank space with rough stone walls, furnished with nothing more than a straw pallet on a hard dirt floor. However, Alexandra had contrived to make her hermitage quite cozy. A two-story cabin of axe-hewn boards and uncemented stones, with two small gaps for windows, had been added to the front of the cave. This ramshackle structure looked to have been thrown together in the dark by a drunken carpenter, but when they stepped through the doorway of rough boards bound together with strips of bark, the room inside was surprisingly pleasant. The outer room, warmed by an open fire, appeared to serve as both kitchen and study. Colourful Tibetan carpets covered the floor, and Buddhist scrolls hung on the walls. For furniture, there were some piled up wooden chests and a low table painted red and gold upon which rested a polished copper bowl. A curtain, brightly patterned in blue and gold and crimson, concealed an inner bedchamber, and upstairs, said Alexandra, clearly proud of her makeshift eyrie, was a guest room and storage space.

Next door was a hut for the servants. *Servants?* wondered Sophie with amusement. But she supposed that French lady hermits fully occupied with meditation and religious studies must have helpers to cook their meals and fetch wood for their fires.

Jeannie had shown Sophie photographs of the young Alexandra. In one, at twenty, she was a youthful feminist in plain dark skirt and severe high necked blouse; in another, a middle-aged, married woman, inclined to matronly plumpness in a stylish suit and enormous chapeau. But Alex's favourite photo was taken in Alexandra's days as a chanteuse with the Opéra Comique. Elaborately costumed in silk and pearls for the role of Thaïs, this Alexandra was sweet-faced, with a girlish prettiness. Her lips wore a mysterious half-smile, and her dark, luminous, almond-shaped eyes held a look of faint wonderment or surprise.

The years had changed Alexandra much more than they had changed Jeannie. Jeannie had the kind of strong-boned face that, apart from the lines of experience around mouth and eyes, did not alter very much between youth and middle age. In this older, plainer, weatherworn Alexandra, youthful prettiness had long since faded.

But then, in honour of their visit, she took from a chest a female lama's robe she had been given by the Sikkimese monks; and when she emerged from her curtained bedchamber dressed in a dark red felt robe with a fringed yellow waistband, high Tibetan leather boots and a bonnet of gold-coloured silk, she took on all the dignity and presence of a lamina.

Presently a small, studious looking youth wearing rimless spectacles and a monk's robe entered the room. He was carrying a large earthenware jug and a tray of wooden drinking bowls. "And this is my son, Yongden," said Alexandra. Yongden set down the tray, bowed politely to each of the guests in turn, and began to hand round the bowls.

Jeannie was staring at Alexandra, her tea-bowl suspended in mid-air. "I was not aware . . . "

"My adopted son," explained Alexandra, smiling at Jeannie's bewilderment. "Or soon to be legally adopted, when the paperwork can be arranged. Yongden is Sikkimese. He is an excellent scholar and a great assistance to me in my writing. He hopes one day to become a lama."

Sophie held out her bowl to Yongden and he filled it with a thick oily black brew bearing scant resemblance to tea. She took a cautious sip. It tasted of rancid butter, and salt, and old tea leaves boiled for days. There was scum floating on top.

"Yak butter tea," said Alexandra. "In this climate, I find it very sustaining."

And an acquired taste, thought Sophie. Unfortunately, each time she managed to a swallow a mouthful, Yongden rushed over to refill her bowl.

"We were so sorry to hear the sad news about your friend the Maharajah," said Jeannie.

A shadow passed across Alexandra's face. "It was a dreadful blow," she said. "I will be a long time recovering from his death."

"In your letter," said Jeannie, "you wrote, if I remember correctly, of strange and inexplicable circumstances. But I understood that he died of a heart attack."

"Supposedly following on jaundice," said Alexandra. "But he did not have jaundice, and his heart was perfectly sound. He was suffering from nothing worse than a minor digestive upset. I often have those myself. His stepmother Queen Drolma called in a Bengali physician employed by the British. When Sidkeong complained of the cold, the physician gave him a huge dose of brandy, piled great numbers of blankets on top of him, and kept a brazier burning beneath his bed. He died within an hour."

Jeannie said "I cannot believe that a young healthy man could die in an hour of overheating and too much brandy."

"Nor can I," said Alexandra. "Nor could anyone. And it was no easy death."

"How do you know all this, Alexandra?"

"One of the Gomchen's servants has a sister who works at the palace. She tells of vomiting, dizziness, shortness of breath, frothing at the mouth . . . "

Sophie's stomach gave a sudden lurch. A chill ran down her spine. *Nausea, dizziness, shortness of breath. Stifling heat.* Surely it was Prince Sidkeong's agony she had shared as she stood on the threshold of that haunted palace room. Her hands trembled as she set down her tea bowl; dark oily liquid sloshed into her lap. Yongden rushed to her side, holding out a cloth. Dabbing absently at her skirt, Sophie looked up and met Alexandra's intent and thoughtful gaze.

"Alex," said Alexandra, turning to the girl. "Do you have your plant book with you?"

For answer Alex unfastened her pack and produced a well thumbed edition of Hooker's *Illustrations of Himalayan Plants.*

"I have some matters to discuss with Mlle. Sophie, which you will find dull. However, if you go a little further up the hillside you may discover some intriguing plants hiding among the rocks. Why don't you take your book and see if you can identify them? Yongden will go with you."

"My dear Sophie," said Alexandra, once the three women were alone, "Jeannie has written to say that you are having visions." She spoke matter-of-factly, as though to have visions was a quite unremarkable event.

Sophie felt her chest tighten. She was not ready to talk about what she had seen in those visions — certainly not to this eccentric stranger. The memory of those episodes filled her with a vague sense of shame, as though it was some flaw in her own nature, some hitherto unsuspected madness that made her a witness to past horrors. But she could see that Alexandra was waiting for an answer. *This*, thought Sophie, *is a patient woman. Patient, and uncompromising.* How else could she have endured this harsh hermit's existence, freezing in a cave in the Himalayan winter, apart for years from her husband, and the comforts of Parisian life, so that she could one day wear the red robe of a lamina?

"And the things you have seen — they frighten you?" prompted Alexandra.

"They terrify me." Sophie met the other woman's calm, penetrating gaze. "They would terrify anyone."

"I too have had visions, Sophie. I have been haunted by invisible beings who tried to drive me away from this country, who said I must give up my Lamaist studies and never attempt to travel in Tibet. I was told these were hallucinations, the result of fever, or brain fatigue, or my tendency to neurasthenia. But no calming drugs ever relieved me of the terror caused by these apparitions."

"Then you understand . . . " Sophie started to say.

But Alexandra, it seemed, was merely leading up to her point. "These visions are not always a curse, Sophie. It can be a gift — the ability to transcend time, to see beyond the veils between the worlds."

"But what I see is terrible."

"Because in this world you have endured terrible experiences, and they will forever be a part of you. But with this gift you have, it is also possible to see wonders. When I was not much older than you, my search for the *inconnu,* the world beyond the world, consumed me, and it came near to destroying me. It is only here in these mountains that I found what I had so desperately yearned for."

"But," said Sophie, almost too softly to be heard, "I am not like you, Madame David-Neel."

"Are you not, *ma chérie?*"

"I only want . . . I want to be ordinary. I want an ordinary life." It was not the right word, but it would have to do.

"So you wish to be commonplace. But you can never be that. You have not had a commonplace life."

No, thought Sophie sadly. *Ordinary girls read romantic novels and go to debutante balls, and marry rich but ordinary men. They live in the present, and the horrors of the past do not intrude upon them.*

"You must not fear your gift, *chérie.* You must explore it. Any talent, not properly understood, unmastered, is a curse to its owner — a torment."

As Alexandra spoke, she glanced briefly at Jeannie, and Sophie caught a glint of wry acknowledgment in Jeannie's eyes. But there was a look of wariness as well.

Eighteen

On their third morning at the hermitage, Alexandra proposed an early ramble on the mountainside. "I want to show you the first glitter of the sun," she said, "on Kanchenjunga's peaks." Pocketing some rolls of film, she added, "Later Alex and I will indulge our botanical interests, and photograph some plant specimens."

Sophie ventured to the doorway of the cave and stepped outside. The air was chill and grey, the sun not yet risen, and a raw wind blew down from the heights. She gazed up at the bleak grey landscape. "I believe," she said, "that I will stay in today and read a book."

"Very wise of you," said Jeannie. "And I believe I'll keep you company." Alex, always keen for adventure, put on her boots, wrapped herself up in a warm jacket, woolly hat, and several scarves, and set off with Alexandra, both of them in high spirits. Yongden trudged after them, laden with Alexandra's camera and tripod.

❧

"Let's put the kettle on," said Jeannie. She dug into her pack and brought out a small tin box of Earl Grey tea. "They won't be back for hours — and Sophie, there are some things we really need to discuss." She put out a few of Alexandra's hard biscuits on a plate, and while the kettle boiled, they piled some cushions by the fire. Jeannie poured the tea into two chipped and saucerless china cups — "No milk, no sugar, I'm afraid" — and then she said, "Alex and I will be going back to Gangtok in a day or two. But Alexandra tells me that she has invited you to stay on."

"For a few weeks, yes. Until we all return to Darjeeling. Would you mind, Jeannie, if I did?"

Jeannie hesitated for a moment. "Actually, we may not be returning to Darjeeling. Tom may be joining us in Gangtok instead. But Sophie," — her face was troubled — "that's not what I wanted to talk to you about."

Oh dear, thought Sophie. Had she done something wrong? Offended against some Indian taboo no one had thought to warn her about?

"I wrote to Alexandra," said Jeannie, "simply asking for advice. I thought she might have some insight into these strange experiences of yours. What should I call them? Visions? Trances? — At any rate, Alexandra has made a study of things that lie outside ordinary experience. It was advice I wanted, Sophie. Only that. I never wished to see you drawn into this peculiar life she's created for herself."

"I don't think . . . " Sophie started to say, but Jeannie was not finished.

"Sophie, my dear, we may laugh about Alexandra's obsessions, Tom and I — but when I knew her in Paris they were real enough, and certainly nothing to laugh about. She seems to have overcome the demons of her youth — the melancholia, the obsessive thoughts that troubled her so much. But too often people like Alexandra will replace one kind of demon with another. Do you remember what she wrote us about her admiration for the Gomchen, in his necklace of skulls and his apron of carved human bones?

Sophie nodded. "She said he was a powerful sorcerer, who supposedly could fly, and command demons, and kill people at a distance. And she hoped he might teach her the secrets of Tantric Buddhism."

"Then keep that in mind, when I show you the kind of book that Alexandra has been studying." Jeannie set down her teacup, got up from her nest of cushions, and fetched a heavy leather-bound volume from the top of a chest. She handed it to Sophie.

Sophie looked down the gilt lettering on the cover. In the dim light she could just make out the title: *The Buddhism of Tibet, or Lamaism*, by L. Austine Waddell.

"Alexandra has marked some pages I thought you should read."

Sophie opened the book and flipped through the pages. The print was too small and dense to read by firelight, so she carried it to the mouth of the cave. Some of the pages were marked with strands of coloured threads. She opened to the first of these and read aloud to Jeannie:

By means of mystic formulas and mantras, one can reach a state of mental fixity whence would result in endowment with supernatural miracle-working power. These miraculous powers may be used for exorcism and sorcery . . .

She flipped through the pages to other markers.

Each Lama has a tutelary demon who accompanies him wherever he goes and guards his footsteps from the minor fiends . . . Dwelling in an atmosphere of superstition, the Lamas, like the alchemists of old, do not recognize the limitations of their powers over nature. They believe that the hermits in their cells, and the monks in their cloisters, can readily become adepts in the black arts, and can banish drought, and control the sun, and stay the storm . . .

She looked up from the page.

"So you see," said Jeannie. "Lamaism, at least as they practise it in these mountains, is deeply rooted in Bon — the old shamanist beliefs and rituals. This may sound very strange — and Sophie, you may think me mad if you wish — but I worry that Alexandra has become fascinated by those ancient, demon-worshipping practices. I wonder now if I've made a mistake in bringing you here. *They do not recognize the limitations of their powers over nature* — that line when I read it filled me with apprehension. No one should seek that kind of power, Sophie. All I can do is to warn you — you must make your own choices. But Alexandra it seems to me is on a very dangerous path."

What an odd turn this conversation had taken, with its talk of black arts, and shamanism, and sorcerers. Yet Jeannie was not given to flights of fancy. Sophie knew that Alexandra in her restless and extraordinary life had been many things — student, *chanteuse*, bourgeois matron, traveller, anarchist perhaps. But demon-worshipper? The thought was so incongruous she wondered if Jeannie was entirely serious. And yet she could see the very genuine concern in Jeannie's face.

"But — do you worry about her influence on Alex?

"Alex is Tom's daughter. She lives very much in the real world. It's Alexandra's difference that interests Alex. She is something to be studied, like an exotic plant — not someone to be emulated. I see no danger to Alex — but to you, Sophie..."

"Was Alexandra a danger to you?"

Jeannie's smile was rueful. "If your dearest friend can be a danger — yes. If she is dear enough to you, that you're willing to follow her wherever she leads. I followed Alexandra into a place where, had I been older and wiser, I would never have chosen to go."

෪

They recognize no limits to their power — the phrase haunted Sophie long after that conversation ended. What did those words mean to Jeannie, and why did they frighten her so much?

And what a strange friendship they shared, this ill-matched pair: Jeannie Grenville-Smith, with her Scotswoman's steadiness and common sense, doing her best to conform to the claustrophobic rules of this still-Victorian world; and Alexandra, to whom the rules, it seemed, were mere inconveniences, to be ignored altogether if they interfered with her plans.

And yet was Jeannie entirely what she seemed? There were the novels that — at least according to Aunt Constance — were unsuitable reading for a young girl. There were the unexplained meetings, the conversations cut off at Sophie's approach; the notebook that seemed to contain research for something other than a novel. There were the veiled hints of something strange in Jeannie's past; and the glances between Jeannie and Alexandra, as though they shared some special knowledge. There was much more about Jean Grenville-Smith that Sophie had yet to learn.

In the meantime, Sophie had her own demons to face. They were pulling her down into a dark place from which she saw no means of escape. She knew that Jeannie, who was kind and sensible, would do anything in her power to protect Sophie from harm. But how could she battle the growing darkness in Sophie's mind?

Jeannie could not help. Alexandra was not sensible; she might or might not be kind, but she knew about things that lay outside ordinary experience; she too had battled demons.

That night, lying sleepless on her makeshift bed of rugs and cushions, Sophie thought, *I need to do this.* To learn from Alexandra how to face with courage those things that terrified her most, to seek in the midst of this enormous emptiness and silence the same quietude of spirit that Alexandra had found.

But then she thought with a sudden chill, supposing Jeannie was right? What if instead of vanquishing her demons, Alexandra had chosen to embrace them?

Nineteen

"IT BEGINS," SAID ALEXANDRA, "WITH solitude. With solitude — and with silence. A space without distraction, in which to observe and to reflect."

They were sitting together on a roughhewn bench just outside Alexandra's cave. Above them, barren mountain slopes rose to the forbidden passes of Tibet. Below were miles of rhododendron forests, and a steep path threading its way through far-off hills and valleys, back to the inhabited world. Close by, prayer flags fluttered; loose pebbles, dislodged by the wind or the feet of some small animal, skittered over the rocks. The only other sound was the distant roar of a waterfall.

A place more solitary than this? More silent?

Alexandra looked at Sophie and smiled, as though reading her thoughts. "For you, I think something less austere than you may be imagining. My attic guestroom will serve well enough at first. No one will disturb you, and your meals will be waiting outside your door. And of course, *par nécessité,* you may walk outside whenever you wish. If any of us catch sight of you, we will pretend you are invisible!"

So there was to be no dark and lonely hermit's cave, no meditation on an icy cliff top. No mention of sorcery or the calling up of demons. Reassuring though this was, it was also oddly disappointing. Alexandra sounded for the entire world like a kindly British governess setting forth a schoolroom schedule.

"But something is puzzling you, *chérie.* I see the drawn-together brows."

"It's only that . . . Jeannie had some concerns. I know she was not happy about letting me stay. There were things in your book . . . "

"*Ah, oui!* You were reading *that* book. Well, that is just one of many books I have been studying. There is much that Professor Waddell knows about Tibet — and much that perhaps he does not. I am making my own study of the subject, for I too intend to write a book."

She tossed a handful of yak dung on the small outdoor cook-fire where Yongden was boiling water to make *tsampa.* (Sadly, the treats that Jeannie had brought from Darjeeling had long since been devoured.) "We have had a long discussion, Jeanne and I, and I hope I have set her mind at rest. I have promised I will not lead you anywhere that it is not safe for you to go."

And Sophie thought how closely those words echoed Jeannie's own: *I followed Alexandra into a place where, had I been older and wiser, I would never have chosen to go.*

Alexandra had assumed that earnest and intent expression she so often wore when she spoke of Buddhism. "What I have explained to Jeanne, and what you must understand, is that there are two paths to enlightenment. There is what the mystics call the Short Path, which is just as it sounds — a path that leads straight up the side of a mountain. It frees the initiate from all the ordinary rules of discipline — but he must be prepared to climb the sheer face of cliffs and cross abysses on a frail rope bridge. It is the path of a few learned scholars who accept the risks of madness and death to achieve the dizzying heights of understanding."

"Like the Gomchen?"

"*Précisemént.* Like the Gomchen, who is my trusted guide and mentor. But understand it is also the path of sorcerers and magicians and charlatans who think that the freedom of the Short Path allows them to engage in dangerous experiments. Those are the lamas Waddell describes, who invite the help of gods and demons to achieve their dubious aims."

Meanwhile, Yongden was pouring yak butter tea into a *tsampa* bowl. He dropped in a handful of barley flour, and bowing politely, handed it to Sophie. Absentmindedly she stirred and kneaded the contents, which as usual were turning into a sticky mess. She set aside the bowl. "Madame David-Neel, which path have you chosen?"

Alexandra gave her a cryptic smile. "If one is wise, one considers all options. But the Short Path is not for you, *chère* Sophie. If you will accept my guidance, we'll begin with some simple meditations, a period of inward-gazing, a removal from all worldly distractions: first steps, on a longer and slower path."

※

In the attic room there was a sleeping rug, a narrow table made from a board set on flat stones, some storage chests. There was no window, but daylight and cold air filtered through cracks in the walls.

Sophie sat with hands resting on knees, ankles crossed under her loose woolen skirt. She could not manage the ankles resting on thighs position that seemed so easy for Alexandra.

They began with breathing exercises — long slow indrawn breaths, deep into the centre of the body, and long slow exhalations — "to calm the mind," Alexandra said. And then — towards sunset on that first day — "Now you must empty your mind of thought."

Sophie could not imagine how this could be done. To think about not thinking — surely that too was a thought? But Alexandra set a small smooth white stone in the centre of the wooden bench, and told Sophie to stare at it, eyes open, until she was able to see it clearly, still, when her eyes were shut. "Concentrate on the image, the after-image, of the stone. Thought does not exist. You do not exist. Nothing but the stone exists. You have become the stone."

Sophie had not realized how hard it was to sit perfectly still for hours at a time. Though she managed to keep her eyes focused on the stone, her thoughts darted everywhere. First her nose began to itch, and then an annoying spot between her shoulders impossible to reach. Somewhere in the room an insect buzzed. From sitting so long cross-legged, her leg muscles cramped.

The last of the filtered light was fading when Alexandra appeared at the top of the ladder. Wincing with pain, Sophie got awkwardly to her feet. "Madame David-Neel, I don't think I can do this. My mind flies everywhere."

"Of course it does," said Alexandra, with neither surprise nor sympathy in her voice. "That is what minds do. That is why you must persist. If you do not master your thoughts, they will master you."

"But everything distracts me . . . "

Alexandra was not listening. "These are simple exercises — the first ones that novices must learn." There was a severity in her tone, a sternness, that Sophie had not heard before. This was a voice not meant to be disobeyed.

Sophie persisted. The pain of long sitting grew less — or perhaps she no longer noticed it. At the end of the third day she had managed to achieve, after a fashion, what Alexandra called "one-pointedness," that state of intense, unwavering concentration, when there was no space for other thought; when her consciousness and all of her being had shrunk to the dimensions of a small round white stone.

"It's a beginning," said Alexandra. "In time you'll learn to concentrate on any object — a tree, a flower, a candle-flame — and everything ceases to exist except that object. You become that tree, that star, that flower, that flame."

After four days — chilled through, aching and stiff from hours of motionless concentration — Sophie thought she had grasped what Alexandra meant. She had become the stone.

I can do this, she thought. And wondered why Jeannie had been so concerned.

ℬ

"Today you will release your thoughts, let them run free and carry you where they will." So saying, Alexandra, with surprising agility for a woman of her age and girth, disappeared down the ladder to the lower room. Sophie was left alone to ponder these instructions.

Let loose your thoughts, let them run free. Did Alexandra realize how long had it been since Sophie had dared to do that? She sat for a while breathing slowly in and out as she had been taught. She could hear the snap and crackle of Yongden's cooking fire; the wind whistling among the rocks; the distant rush of water. Random images, old anxieties, broken strands of memory drifted into her mind, lingered for a moment, and dissolved.

Her first sight of imperial Calcutta's fading glory — white walls, green spaces, noise and blossoming trees and dirt and swamp-smell . . . a poem to a dead girl in an ancient graveyard . . . the night of Kali, the sky lit up by fire . . .

Don't think of Calcutta. There was danger there. Go back in time, in space, go back to childhood. There, locked away in the English countryside, were the safe memories, the happy ones.

. . . fallen apples in the yellow autumn grass . . . a winter fireside, flames reflected in a crystal wineglass, the glow of lamplight gilding her mother's hair . . . waking to the first snowfall, a hushed, immaculate world (if they wintered in these mountains, would she see snow again?) . . . those long afternoons with a book on a cushioned bench in the summerhouse, or in the conservatory while rain beat against the glass . . . but no, not rain, surely that was the sound of waves . . .

. . . jolted out of sleep in a narrow bunk, a ripping sound like torn cotton, a frantic hammering on the cabin door . . .

Her throat clenched; there was a strange plunging sensation in her stomach. Cold ran down her spine like icy fingers. As panic seized her body, her mind retreated, flinching away from the monstrous shadow blotting out the horizon, obliterating all other thoughts.

Darkness. The air frigid, the sea an infinite expanse of black glass. The sky glittering with stars. The dark, the bitter cold, the sickening awareness of unthinkable loss. The ship's stern a monstrous finger pointing skyward, its ghostly lights still glimmering beneath the water. The music slow and sombre now, a familiar hymn. And then that terrible rising din of voices.

This was the place she would always come to. There was no way around it and no way across.

Twenty

"A s Buddhists, Sophie, we learn that all is illusion."

"Illusion?" Sophie felt the colour rise to her face. When had she become so quick to anger? The words were out before she could think to choke them back: "My parents are dead. They fell into the sea and they drowned. I survived, and they are dead, and no amount of wishing can change that."

"*Chère* Sophie," said Alexandra softly, "I know, in your world, in the material world, that is true, and we can only hope that time will make it easier for you. But when you relive the experience, again, and again, that is a waking dream, that is illusion."

"But it was not a dream! I've dreamt of that night, more times than I can count, and woke up, and knew I'd been dreaming. But this time, I was *there*." Sophie's heart was racing now. She could hear the shrillness in her voice, the anger and indignation. She felt betrayed by Alexandra, betrayed too by Jeannie, who had been so sure that Alexandra would understand. "I felt our lifeboat rock and pitch, felt someone's hand grip mine, felt a blanket thrown round my shoulders. My teeth were chattering so hard that my jaw ached. I smelled salt and rope and canvas." *Just as I smelled rotting flowers when I stood on the blood-drenched floor in the Kali temple — as I felt the fever and sickness, the poison in my own blood, in the room where Prince Sidkeong died.*

Another woman, certainly any English memsahib, might have rebuked Sophie for this outburst, gazed at her askance for her raised voice, the lack of proper respect in her tone. But Alexandra's broad weatherworn face remained untroubled.

"Sophie, do not distress yourself. I comprehend what you are feeling. What you have experienced is not easily explained. If not dream, if not illusion, what?" Then she said, "There was a woman I once knew who would have given you another, perhaps a better, explanation."

Sophie waited, not trusting herself to speak. She breathed in slowly, deeply, and as slowly breathed out. Gradually, the thudding of her heart quieted.

Alexandra said "Her name was Helena Petrovna Blavatsky. Perhaps Jeannie has told you of her?"

Sophie let out another long, deep breath. She felt able to speak calmly now. "Yes, of course. The famous HPB. When Jeannie was young and living in London, she worked as Madame Blavatsky's assistant."

"And what has Jeannie told you?"

"Not a great deal. She seems to remember her fondly, though she says she was very eccentric, and not an easy taskmistress."

Alexandra smiled at that. "An understatement, I think. *En tout cas*, HPB had a great many devoted followers who shared her theosophical beliefs. She wrote some enormous books, which to my way of thinking made no sense at all. A vast expenditure of ink to no great end."

It was Sophie's turn to smile. "That's more or less what Jeannie said."

"However, part of HPB's teaching was that above and beyond our real, material world there is another plane of existence, the astral plane. Each of us has another self, a kind of spirit double that can travel on that other plane, connected only by a thin silver cord, while our physical self remains behind. Thus, according to the Theosophists, we enter a zone where neither space nor time has meaning, so that we can move freely through both space and time."

For Sophie, this had echoes of eccentric theories published in cheap paper-covered pamphlets — ley lines, the hidden continent of Mu, the lost secrets of Atlantis. And travelling through time was one of those imaginary things that happened to people in books by Mr. Wells. She could hear her father's voice saying, "Poppycock!" He had no more patience with such stories, than with photographs of fairies in English gardens. Yet Alexandra was speaking as matter-of-factly as a teacher giving a geometry lesson. (Hadn't Tom once said that Alexandra, like the White Queen, could believe six impossible things before breakfast?)

And was any of this less possible than what she had already experienced? For Sophie Pritchard the world had long since ceased to be explicable.

"Madame David-Neel — is that what *you* believe?"

Alexandra hesitated. She said, as though weighing her words, "I have no reason to *disbelieve* it. A belief in planes of existence beyond our own goes back to the ancient Greeks — perhaps to the beginning of humankind. *Chère* Sophie, what a skeptical look you give me! But I have read many accounts of out-of-body travel, and I've been told first hand of such experiences — of details recalled, of conversations overheard in rooms where the person has never been. It can happen through deep meditation or in that twilight state on the edge of sleep." And then, looking closely at Sophie, she said, "I've read that experiencing a great shock can also cause the astral self to separate from the physical body."

A great shock. Was Alexandra offering her, finally, the awful truth? Sophie thought with sorrow of that other self, her shadow self, ripped apart from her by terror and grief — a sad ghost-girl cast adrift in time.

The late afternoon light was fading. "You're shivering," said Alexandra. "Come inside."

In the shelter of the cave, Alexandra found matches and lit the kerosene lamp. Sophie watched her face in the lamp's glow — the well-worn, unremarkable face of a woman without vanity and without pretence. Her short, sturdy figure, shapeless in its brown robe, was an oddly reassuring presence. But there was still a tremour of fear creeping down Sophie's spine, and a terrible question that needed to be asked.

"Madame David Neel, if you can travel into the past, if time has no meaning, does that mean you might also travel into the future?"

Alexandra set down the lamp and turned her attention to the primus stove. "I have met lamas who seem to have that ability, though they seldom talk about it."

But that would be a dreadful thing, thought Sophie. "To see death? The death of people you love? To see your own death?"

"It might not be death that you see."

"But it *is* what I see. It's what I always see. And to experience what lies ahead, before it happens — I couldn't bear it."

Alexandra was setting out the cups for butter tea. "I know of no lama who has foreseen his own death. Perhaps because the future is infinitely mutable, as the past is not. The manner of one's death is not fixed but random. It depends on too many variables to easily predict. We change our minds, take the high path and not the lower one, and the earthquake strikes. Do we live or die? It rests on a split second decision. Or our foot slips on a loose stone and we tumble into the abyss."

"Then it is all nonsense, what HPB taught? We cannot see into the future?"

"Perhaps we cannot. But consider, Sophie — some outcomes are not random. There are some that are planned, that will inevitably take place if nothing interferes with the logical progression of events. Do this, and this, and this next will follow." While she waited for the kettle to boil, Alexandra had settled comfortably into lecture mode. "We do not see the mechanisms at work, are not aware of plans laid, schemes devised, the slow and careful progress towards disaster. Suppose one *could* travel freely through time and space — could observe those schemes and mechanisms, could track their progress, foresee their outcome. Then perhaps catastrophe — even death — could be averted."

Glancing impatiently at the kettle, Alexandra interrupted herself to pump the primus. Then: "What you have can be a curse, *chérie*. I would never deny that. But there could be power in it too, the kind of power that can come with foreknowledge. I have always placed a high value on knowledge, regardless of the cost."

As she said this, there was a certain look in her eyes, a hint of self-mockery in the quirk of her mouth. Sophie was reminded of what this plain, stout, aging woman once had been — *une petite sauvage*, a youthful anarchist; a rebellious Parisienne with a thirst for adventure and a head full of mad schemes.

TWENTY-ONE

FOR SOPHIE, AS IT HAD for Alexandra, the silence and solitude of the mountains began to work its magic. Together they went on long tramps over windswept ridges and boulder-strewn heights, across waterfalls and into high valleys filled with chains of glassy turquoise lakes. More than once they climbed to the northern frontier. Beyond those passes lay the vast Tibetan tableland — that mysterious country Alexandra so passionately wished to explore.

But there was no more talk of astral travel — nor ever any mention of sorcerers and demons. If Alexandra continued to study that arcane part of Tibetan belief, she did not speak of it to Sophie. Instead, she taught her mantras, meditations, breathing exercises designed to quiet her troubled spirit and lead it into a calm, silent place.

"Imagine a lotus flower," Alexandra would say. "On each of the petals, imagine a holy figure, a Bodhisattva, and one Bodhisattva stands at the very heart of the flower. Then as the lotus begins to fold its petals, each one emits a ray of light . . ." Or Sophie was to fill a small bowl of water up to the brim, and try to carry it across the room without spilling a drop. "It's an exercise to test the tranquility of your mind," said Alexandra. "If there is any trace of sadness, or memory, or desire, or even joy in your mind, your body will know, and the water will surely spill out." On the last day before she was to leave the hermitage, Sophie managed to carry the bowl from one side of the room to the other without a drop of water spilled.

ॐ

In early summer, Thekong came to fetch Sophie back to Gangtok. On the morning of their departure Sophie sat with Alexandra for one last time on the bench outside the hermitage, drinking for politeness's sake a cup of Yongden's butter tea, and saying her farewells.

She was eager to see Jeannie and Alex again, and Tom, too, when he came to join them. But, seized by a sudden awful uncertainty, she thought, *am I truly ready to go out into the world? To deal with these powers I seem to possess, without Alexandra to reassure me?*

But Alexandra, as usual, seemed to read her thoughts. She said, "Before you go, Sophie, I will tell you a story an old lama once told to me. Somewhere in the Himalayas there is a village lying at the foot of a high peak where people are very careful always to observe the position of the sun, for at certain times of year, the shadow of the summit falls across the valley like a finger of darkness. The villagers believe that if anyone is caught in that shadow, terrible misfortune is sure to befall them. You were caught in the shadow of the mountain, Sophie, but that is in the past and it's time for you to come out into the sunlight." She pressed her weathered brown cheek to Sophie's. "I have taught you as well as I can, *chérie*," she said softly. "Now go with my love and my blessing."

ॐ

106

In Gangtok, Sophie found Jeannie and Alex settled into a pleasant hillside bungalow, as they awaited Tom's arrival.

Though Gangtok was not much larger than a village, and the small English colony mostly composed of missionaries, it was an important trading depot, the crossroads of many kingdoms. On market days Sophie spent hours wandering with Lily and Alex through the maze of narrow alleys lined with booths and kiosks selling scrolls and prayer wheels, jewelry, spices and tea and chili peppers, intricately patterned carpets from Tibet, shimmering lengths of jewel-coloured silk. The air was rich with the scent of cardamom, loud with horns and kettledrums and the babble of many languages. There were Bhutia people from northern Sikkim, the men in long claret coloured robes with wide loose sleeves, the women wearing heavy necklaces of gold and silver filigree set with turquoise. There were Lepchas, the native inhabitants of Sikkim, in striped homespun cotton, their hair in pigtails, their long straight swords suspended from their belts. Red-robed lamas twirled prayer-wheels; Tibetan horsemen rode by on silver-inlaid saddles with harness bells jingling and scarves floating in the wind. Mingling as well in the crowded aisles were Sherpas and Indians and Bhutanese, and uniformed Nepalese soldiers, the famous Gurkha.

Lily was frightened by the Gurkhas, with their sharp-edged wickedly curving *kukris,* but Alex was rapt with admiration. "They're fighting for England and our King," she told Lily. "If I had a *kukri* — perhaps just a small one — then I could defend you and Sophie if ever you were attacked."

"I expect you could," said Sophie, smiling.

But Lily said firmly, "It's new sandals you'll be needing, not weapons, Miss Memsahib," and led her off to the shoemaker's booth.

In the afternoons, there were visitors to tea — both English and Sikkimese — and because the Grenville-Smiths were friends of Sir Charles and Lady Bell, there were frequent invitations to dine out. Now conversation inevitably turned to the war in Europe and in the Middle East. People spoke with dismay of the Turkish campaign at Gallipoli, with its appalling casualties. At home in England, German zeppelins were dropping bombs on the eastern counties. The Sikkimese peasants, said Lady Bell with ill-concealed anger, were resisting conscription, but thousands of Gurkhas and other hill people had volunteered to fight on the British side. The Dalai Lama had offered to send a thousand Tibetan soldiers to fight for England, but regretted that he could not provide them with rifles, for there were not a thousand rifles in all of Tibet, and with the Chinese invaders still on their border they could not spare the few they had. And then there was talk of the German mission that had made its way from Romania to Constantinople disguised as a travelling circus. Fortunately the rifles and machine guns — and wireless equipment disguised as tent-poles — that followed them by rail, had been seized by a suspicious Romanian customs officer.

One afternoon, Jeannie invited to tea a young relative of the Bells. Invalided out of his regiment with a leg wound, Will Fitzgibbon had been sent to convalesce in the hills of Sikkim instead of an English hospital. He had just turned twenty-two — a tall, lean youth with fair English skin that had reddened but not tanned in the Indian sun. His eyes were the colour of cornflowers, but they were circled by dark shadows. When he lifted his teacup Sophie saw that his hand shook so that he had to set it down again.

Sophie was reminded of how much she missed the company of those young Oxford and Cambridge men who, when she had lived at home in Sussex, came to stay with their families on neighbouring estates. She had been thirteen years old in the golden summer of 1911 — a summer that seemed it would never end. That year there were more young men than usual spending their long holidays in the blissful English countryside, instead of embarking on their customary jaunts to Europe, where rumours of war were gathering strength. They had obligingly turned out in boaters and blazers to fêtes and garden parties, and they had played the part of older brothers for Sophie, who had no brothers of her own. They cheerfully vanquished her at tennis and let her defeat them at croquet. Will Fitzgibbon might have been one of those dashing young undergraduates who, three years later, went blithely off to war with no more thought, it seemed to Sophie, than if it were just another cricket match.

Will had the good looks and easy manners of those young men, but something had gone missing. There should not have been such flatness in his eyes. Sophie knew that look, and had seen it in the eyes of women survivors who had stood shivering with her on the deck of the Carpathia — women dazed and bereft and terribly grieving, spared against all odds from death at sea. She knew that emptiness must have been in her own eyes those first terrible months.

"Did you serve in France, like Major Bradley?" asked Alex, eager for details.

Will glanced at her with a faint smile that did not reach his eyes. "In Flanders," he said, and turned back to his meal, pushing his food absentmindedly into the centre of his plate. Sophie realized he had not eaten any of it.

That evening, when Alex had gone off to bed and Sophie was alone with Jeannie in the sitting room, she asked, "What happened to Will in Flanders, Jeannie? It was more than just a leg wound, wasn't it?"

Jeannie put down her book. She said, very quietly, "They were defending the British lines a few miles from Ypres. Just before a bullet hit Will, he saw his best friend blown to bits before his eyes. He will be a long time getting over that, I think."

Twenty-Two

"Look, Sophie!" Alex rushed out onto the veranda clutching her *Illustrated Dictionary of Herbs*. She was still dressed in a rumpled cotton frock and sandals — though she had been twice told by Lily to change — because Major Bradley was coming to tea.

"Just look!" She held the book out to Sophie, open to a coloured drawing of tall blue flowers.

Sophie glanced down at the page. "That's monkshood," she said. "It grew in our garden at home."

"Sophie, I *know* that it's monkshood." Alex's tone was withering. "And it's *very, very* poisonous. That's why it's also called wolfsbane. And you have to read on the next page where it says 'symptoms of wolfsbane poisoning'."

Sophie took the book from her and scanned down the page. She read, "Nausea, dizziness, vomiting, shortness of breath . . . "

"You see! I saw monkshood growing in the palace garden, that day when we went to tea with the queen. It was her, it was the queen. She poisoned the prince. I knew she was wicked, Sophie."

Oh Alex, thought Sophie, *The poisoned apple, the jealous queen. If you live in a storybook world, the stepmother is always wicked.* "Alex, there are plenty of other things that could cause those symptoms. And if it was poison, whatever makes you think it was the queen?"

"Because," said Alex, "she didn't care that he was dead!"

At that moment Major Bradley appeared at the end of the path.

Before Sophie could think to stop her, Alex marched up to the major, brandishing the book. "She killed Alexandra's friend, Major Bradley. She killed the prince."

"She?" The major gazed down at Alex, clearly caught off guard.

"Queen Drolma. She poisoned the prince. With monkshood."

"Did she indeed? Queen Drolma did that?" Though his voice was amused, Sophie saw his brows draw together, his mouth tighten. Sophie thought, *this comes to him as no surprise.*

"Major Bradley, you must tell the police."

"So, my dear Alex, let me understand what you're saying. You wish me to accuse a member of the Sikkimese royal family of murdering her stepson? Charles Bell will hardly thank me for that."

"But you *don't* understand . . . "

"Indeed I do, my dear Alex. All too well. But there is a great deal you do not understand. And I see by Miss Pritchard's shocked expression that she does not understand either." He was speaking more, now, to Sophie than to Alex. "Prince Sidkeong wanted to reform Buddhism and rid it of superstition — reforms that the rest of the royal family opposed. But he was also seeking independence from Britain — so of course the royal family lays the blame for the prince's death on the British. This is a nest of snakes Sir Charles will have no intention of stirring up."

"But we must tell Alexandra," Alex protested, her face still flushed with excitement and indignation. "We have to tell her who murdered her friend."

"I think you will find," said Major Bradley quietly, "that Mme. David already knows. And she realizes why nothing can be done."

Sophie understood all too well Alex's outrage and disbelief. The world, she decided, was a terribly unjust place, where murderous queens went unpunished, while innocent young men were blown to bits in battle, and blameless travellers plunged to their icy deaths.

Dazzled and bewildered by this unfamiliar world, she was only now beginning to sense how dangerous that world might be. Bombs thrown in a busy Calcutta street, princes assassinated, the all powerful Raj with no power to bring a murderer to justice, and no escape, even in this small remote kingdom, from the horrors of the European war.

Power comes with foreknowledge, Alexandra had said. Could her parents' death, the death of so many others have been foreseen?

Suppose it was true that *Titanic* sank not by a whim of fate, or the will of God, but because of human error — a moment's inattention, excessive speed, a flaw in the design of that supposedly unsinkable vessel, a series of errors and omissions inevitably leading to disaster. If there had been some traveller in the timeless zone where everything has happened and is happening, and is about to happen — could they have seen catastrophe bearing down upon the ship and given the alarm?

She had grown to love this second family. She could not bear the thought of losing them. Was it in her power to keep

Alex safe, and Jeannie, and Tom — if not from random acts of fate, at least from that which happened by intent, or was pre-ordained?

Or was that as improbable a thought as Alex's childish wish for a kukri of her own?

TWENTY-THREE

THE MISSES RANSOME AND ELLIOT from the English mission at Lachen had been invited to dinner at the Bells. Aging expatriate gentlewomen, soft-spoken and sensibly attired, they brought with them a Dr. Llewellyn, who had been staying at the mission as a paying guest. He was a short, portly man of middle age, with a drooping mustache and neatly trimmed grey beard. He was on a year's sabbatical, he told them, from a boys' public school in the Midlands, where he taught the natural sciences.

"And what brings you to Sikkim?" inquired his hostess.

He gave her an ingratiating smile. "Merely an amateur's enthusiasm for ornithology, Lady Bell. These mountains are inhabited with some rare and fascinating birds — more than four hundred species, I'm informed."

Sophie, seated on his right, said, "If you are staying at Lachen, perhaps you have met our friend Madame David-Neel."

Dr. Llewellyn's eyebrows rose in surprise and evident disapproval. "My dear young lady, I must advise you most strongly to stay away from this woman. My friends at the mission tell me that she is known to consort with magicians. Indeed, she may herself indulge in such practices. Whether that is true or not, it's well known that she flagrantly defies both the rules of civilized society and the rule of law."

"I say, that's putting it a bit strong," said Sir Charles. "She's eccentric, true enough. But as to uncivilized — I've found to her to be a clever and well-educated woman, with an impressive knowledge of Tibetan culture."

"There's no need for you to defend her," said Lady Bell, in a slightly acid tone. "She is quite capable of doing that for herself."

"But Sir Charles," said Dr. Llewellyn, "are you not aware of her background? She was known in her youth to have anarchist connections."

Now why would you be interested enough to find that out? wondered Sophie.

"In fact," their guest continued, "I have good reason to believe that the woman is a Russian spy."

A former anarchist working for the Czar of Russia? How very unlikely! Sophie's disbelief must have shown on her face: Will Fitzgibbon, a quiet presence across the table, gave her a quick amused glance.

"I've heard some idle talk," said Sir Charles, smiling faintly. "I've seen no evidence of it."

"But," persisted Dr. Llewellyn, "if she were not working for Russian interests, why would she be so determined to flout the law and cross the border into Tibet?"

But we're no longer at war with Russia, thought Sophie. Then she remembered that while the British could not travel in Tibet without permission, neither could the Russians — and the new alliance with Russia was still an uneasy one. But in any case she had taken a dislike to this pompous little man. She would not want to have been one of his pupils.

Miss Ransome, who until now had been listening quietly, said, "This Gomchen, this sorcerer with whom she consorts — I have seen him in the village. A frightful creature, so grubby, with long greasy hair piled on top of his head, and the manners of a peasant."

"I can't think," added Miss Elliot, "why a respectable woman, presumably of good family, would seek out his company."

"And of course — though one hesitates to mention it — her very close friendship with the late prince Sidkeong," murmured Miss Ransome. "Not that I really believed the talk . . . "

How dare they say such things about Alexandra, when they've never met her? And what right have they to condemn the Gomchen, because his world is different from theirs? Sophie knew it was not her place to speak. Still, she could see Jeannie's look of barely concealed annoyance.

"Moreover," added Miss Ransome, "it is our dearest wish to carry the gospel to the people of Tibet. What right has Madame David-Neel to demand the permission that we have been so unreasonably refused?"

Of course, thought Sophie. *Surely that's what this is all about. They're afraid that Alexandra has influence, and will be permitted to travel in Tibet, when they cannot.*

As the servants removed the soup plates and served the chicken curry, Lady Bell deftly redirected the conversation. "And will you be staying for a while at the Mission, Dr. Llewellyn?"

"Actually, no," he told her. "I've decided to take lodgings in Gangtok instead of returning to Lachen — once the rains come, I fear the mission will be entirely cut off from civilization."

From across the table Sir Charles and Lady Bell exchanged a fleeting glance. Sophie caught the look, but was not sure how to interpret it.

ॐ

In the next day's mail, Jeannie received a note from Dr. Llewellyn, proposing a bird-watching expedition. "It would be a pity to waste this lovely weather," he wrote in elegant copperplate. "Perhaps the young ladies would like to accompany me?"

"Mummy, could we?" Alex had been wistfully suggesting such a foray since their arrival in Gangtok. Jeannie hesitated, seeming a little taken aback.

"Please, Mommy?"

"It's very kind of Dr. Llewellyn to invite you," said Jeannie. "Shall we talk about it later?"

"It's later," Alex announced at dinner, as soon as she had finished her pudding. "We have to talk about our expedition with Dr. Llewellyn,"

"And I have to see if Thekong is available to go with you, "said Jeannie. "I wouldn't dream of sending the two you out into the forest with only Dr. Llewellyn to protect you."

Thekong, who had few enough duties to occupy his time while waiting for Tom to arrive, was only too pleased to act as guide. The forest-dwelling Lepchas, Tom had once said, were born naturalists and philosophers. Sikkimese bred, with Lepcha blood, Thekong clearly longed to revisit the paths he had roamed as a boy.

They set out in light drizzle and early mist for a nearby woodland. At mid-morning the sun broke through, and a watery green light filtered through the forest canopy. The air smelled of rain-wet flowers. In this part of the forest, fragile clusters of orchids — white, yellow, purple, pink — clung to huge moss-covered, vine-garlanded magnolias and oaks. In the clearings there were swarms of butterflies, and pink and blue hydrangeas in bloom.

A rotting log gave way under Sophie's foot and she half-stumbled. Dr. Llewellyn, walking close behind her, caught her arm to steady her. Without conscious thought, she flinched away. Surely the gesture had been well-meant, and yet . . . the lines of an old poem leaped to mind.

I do not like you, Doctor Fell.

The reason why I cannot tell . . .

It was not only because Dr. Llewellyn had offended Jeannie and Alex, speaking so unkindly — and unjustly — of Alexandra. For reasons she could not quite identify, she knew that she would not want to be alone with this man. For the rest of that morning, she stayed close to Thekong and made sure that Alex was always by her side. Still, she need only be civil to Dr. Llewellyn. There would be little necessity for conversation.

They followed the path down a steep slope, and now oak, birch, and maple — the familiar trees of an English wood — gave way to ferns and giant bamboo. The path was carpeted with fallen orchid blossoms. Alex had taken off her sunbonnet and tucked one into her tousled red hair.

"Miss Grenville-Smith, what a charming picture you make," declared Dr. Llewellyn. "You must allow me take a snapshot." And before Sophie could think to respond, he had taken a handheld camera from his pack.

Afterwards, Sophie thought that Jeannie would surely not have allowed Alex's picture to be taken. But how could Sophie have prevented it? The incident made her feel uncomfortable and a little guilty.

"Aha," said Dr. Llewellyn, making an entry in his notebook, "If I am not mistaken, that is a Blood Pheasant. What an excellent sighting, on our first hour out."

Sophie saw Thekong give him an odd look. It was Alex who announced, in a reproving tone, "That wasn't a Blood Pheasant, Dr. Llewellyn."

"Oh, my dear child, surely it was, I saw the markings . . . "

Polite child that she was, Alex did not argue. But later, as she and Sophie walked back with Thekong to the bungalow, she said again, "That wasn't a Blood Pheasant. Was it, Thekong?"

Thekong shook his head.

"An ornithologist would know that," Alex said.

"But he said he was only an amateur bird-watcher," said Sophie. "And I suppose he would be more familiar with English birds."

"Nonetheless," said Alex, "he *ought* to have known. The Blood Pheasant is the state bird of Sikkim. And anyway, it mostly lives at the snowline. You never see it as low as this except in winter."

And Thekong nodded his silent agreement.

❦

Early in June Tom arrived from Calcutta, but was able to stay for only a fortnight before embarking with Thekong on a zoological expedition to the Nepalese border — "looking for snow leopards and giant wild sheep," said Alex knowledgeably.

In these last days of fine weather before the monsoon rains, Jeannie seemed unusually quiet, almost distracted. Sophie guessed that she was missing Tom, after a reunion that proved all too brief, and was anxious for the safety of her elder daughter Diana now that bombing raids on London had begun.

At home and at the British Residency, in the marketplace, at the tennis court where Sophie was improving Alex's skill with a racquet, she caught snatches of conversation. German bombs were falling on Stepney and Spitalfields, and there were terrible casualties in Belgium. A German U-boat had sunk the liner Lusitania off the coast of Ireland. Children were on board and they had perished with over a thousand other passengers. *One hundred and fifty drowned babies.* Hearing that, Sophie felt weak and ill. She knew that image would haunt her for a very long time.

And there were the whispered conversations, the ones she was not meant to overhear — rumours from India of attempted bombings, failed at the eleventh hour, when who knew how many lives had been saved because an informant had been listening at precisely the right place and time.

Sophie strove to keep those rumours from her mind as she practised the exercises Alexandra had taught her. Each day, settling into the lotus position, she concentrated on a small statue of the Buddha she had bought in the market.

Remain motionless and tranquil.

Think not of the past.

Think not of the future.

Think not. I am meditating.

Do not imagine.

Do not reason, do not analyze.

Cease from all effort.

If a thought comes, give it no attention.

Dismiss it from the mind the moment it is born.

Thoughts, images came and went. She let them drift by unexamined. *The tranquil mind observes the uninterrupted flow of ideas, like the passage of a stream.*

On some days she emerged from the solitude of her bedroom with a renewed lightness of spirit, a determination to turn away forever from the past, to await the future without fear, and without anticipation. On those days she truly believed that she was healing.

Then came the reports in weeks-old newspapers of ships sunk and lives lost. Meanwhile, the sound of fife and drums from the parade ground, as the Gurkha Rifles readied for foreign campaigns, reminded her that not even Sikkim could escape the encroaching shadow of war.

The old dreams returned, of death by water; but now, as well, there were dreams of fire, when black smoke engulfed the world and mountains of flame towered against the night sky. Too often she woke with sweat-soaked sheets and a sense of imminent, faceless danger.

Little escaped Jeannie Guthrie's watchful eyes. One day she asked Sophie, "The exercises Alexandra taught you — are they helping you at all?"

"Oh yes," said Sophie, knowing full well it was not the whole truth. She lived at times with nerves so on edge that no breathing exercises, no visualizations could calm her. Sometimes, as she sat undisturbed in her room drawing her breath deep into the centre of her being, she seemed almost to float out of herself and she found herself in an empty place that was full of doors she refused to open, in dread of what might lie behind.

Twenty-Four

ALEX HAD MADE A NEW friend. Darius Mehta was a young Indian from Bombay who had recently taken his degree in natural sciences at Balliol College, Oxford. Now he was in Gangtok as a member of Tom Grenville-Smith's research team, helping to lay the groundwork for the zoological survey of India. That at least was how he explained his presence in Sikkim, though Sophie suspected that he had been asked by Tom to keep a watchful eye on the Grenville-Smith household in Tom and Thekong's absence. Darius called both Sophie and Alex "Miss Memsahib" just as Thekong did, though with a smile that belied the deference in the title.

Alex was instantly smitten, for as she explained to Sophie, he knew everything there was to know about the habits of the snow leopard and the red panda — her favourite Himalayan beasts — and he was always ready to answer her questions. Sophie liked him too, though with more discretion. His unselfconscious charm — and his enthusiasm for cricket — put her fondly in mind of those young Oxford and Cambridge friends of her English childhood.

Returning from the market one Saturday morning Sophie and Alex followed the path that led past the cricket field. A match had just finished as they arrived, and they saw Darius, in white trousers and open-necked white shirt, standing on the pitch. Catching sight of Alex and Sophie he gave them a friendly wave.

"Did you win?" Alex called out as she waved back.

"We did indeed. Hang on a bit while I collect my gear, and I'll walk you home."

They waited for him at the edge of the field. "Sophie," said Alex, in a thoughtful voice, "Don't you think that Darius looks like a prince?"

"A prince? Really?"

"Yes. A Prince of Persia. Like Prince Farouz-Schah in 'The Magic Horse'. Do you suppose he might really be a prince, Sophie?"

"It's hardly likely," said Sophie, smiling. There were plenty of princes in India, and probably several at Oxford, but she knew that Darius was a scholarship student, the son of a minor Bombay civil servant.

�

"You have an interesting name," said Sophie, making polite conversation as they started together up the steep road to the bungalow. "Perhaps you're called after Darius the Great?"

Darius laughed. "After the King of Persia? In a sense, I suppose. All Parsis came originally from Persia, and we all have Persian given names. I dare say my parents had high ambitions for me."

Sophie turned to smile at him. *How very good looking he is!* The thought took her by surprise. Alex was right. With his dark eyes and olive skin, his high-cheekboned, hawk-nosed face, he did look like a prince in a Persian fairy tale.

Such notions would have scandalized Aunt Constance, and upset the Calcutta memsahibs. But somehow in these mountains, at the far edge of the Empire, divisions of race and belief seemed less important. She thought of Alexandra's loving (though surely innocent!) friendship with Prince Sidkeong, her affection for her adopted son Yongden, her deep respect for the Gomchen. How insignificant the colour of one's skin must seem to Alexandra.

There were several books in Sir Charles Bell's library on the Zoroastrian faith of the Parsis. Intrigued, she asked to borrow one. As Darius had explained, his ancestors had taken refuge in India many centuries ago, after the Muslim conquest of Persia. She read with growing interest about the good and wise God Ahura Mazda and his evil opponent Ahriman, about fire rituals, and about the Towers of Silence where the Parsi dead were exposed to the sun and to birds of prey.

If Jeannie noticed Sophie's new interest in cricket, and in books on early Persian history, she failed to comment on it. Lately she had spent most of her days in seclusion — working on her novel, Sophie presumed. When she emerged for dinner, her eyes looked tired and strained.

Days of damp heat and violent thunderstorms had made everyone in the household tense and short-tempered. The monsoon rains arrived at last, crashing on the bungalow roof and pounding against the windows. Torrents of muddy water rushed down the steep lanes. The mountains vanished behind swirling banks of mist, as dense as cotton batting. No one travelled unless they had to. Hillsides slid down upon the roads, especially where the forest had been cleared for teagardens, and roads washed into the swollen river.

Housebound, Sophie and Alex played parlour games, conscripting Lily — and the occasional unwary visitor — to games of twenty questions, and charades, and Consequences.

The rain must have kept Dr. Llewellyn indoors as well, for even on the drier days when they ventured outdoors they seldom encountered him. In the market one day, though, he approached Sophie and Jeannie, catching them by surprise.

"I see, Miss Pritchard," he remarked, "that you are quite friendly with the young Indian from Bombay." He managed to put an emphasis on "friendly" that made Sophie feel embarrassed and uneasy. Then turning to Jeannie, "A word of advice, my dear lady. These educated Indians are not always quite trustworthy."

Jeannie gave him what Sophie thought of as her Enraged-Memsahib look — a glance so scathing that it should have stunned him into silence. But Dr. Llewellyn, seemingly oblivious, carried on: "And your husband, Mrs. Grenville-Smith — were you not expecting him home before the rains began?"

"You must excuse us," said Jeannie curtly. "We really must finish our marketing," and ignoring his question she hurried Sophie and Alex away.

Through the monsoon months, Sophie spent hours each day practising the exercises Alexandra had taught her. Life stilled to a quiet routine of meals, and reading, and meditation, and sleep. But sometimes on nights when the rain battered the roof like waves buffeting a ship's hull, her dreams carried her into a dangerous place from which she awakened sick with dread.

Elsewhere, rumours abounded. German agents in the Persian Gulf, in the guise of diplomats, were said to be stirring up the local tribespeople in a campaign of murderous violence against the British. On the Western Front, a bloody stalemate dragged on, while on the Eastern front, a German offensive was engaged in destroying the Russian army. The German navy continued to sink passenger vessels. Meanwhile, the British newspapers continued to publish upbeat and optimistic military reports.

Once, for a fleeting moment while deep in meditation, Sophie found herself in a dim, lamp-lit space occupied by huddled, faceless figures. It was a place she did not recognize, a room where she knew she had never been.

She did not feel herself physically present in this room. Rather, she was a kind of distant, ghostly onlooker. She sensed, this time, that she was not a witness to the past, but to some danger, some desperate threat that was still to come. And then with a kind of mental wrenching she found herself fully conscious, her heart beating fast, her face damp with perspiration.

Through the rest of that long wet summer, Sophie felt as though she were floating in suspension while she waited for some huge unheralded event that must occur before ordinary life could return.

Twenty-Five

F OR SOME TIME THERE HAD been rumours of smuggled leaflets circulating in the tribal villages of the northwest frontier, praising the German cause and accusing the British of horrible crimes against Islam. Then in early September a courier attempting to cross from Sikkim into Nepal was intercepted by a border patrol, and when they discovered what was in his pack they arrested him on the spot and sent him back to Gangktok to be questioned.

This information came from Lily, who had heard it in the market from a parlourmaid at the British Residency. When Sophie, out of curiosity, asked Jeannie what she thought the courier might have been carrying, the answer was a wary *"pas devant les enfants"* and a quick change of subject. Once they were alone, with Alex safely in bed, Jeannie was a little more forthcoming.

The pale, drawn look that she had acquired over the monsoon months was still apparent as she said, with a wry smile, "There's not much that escapes our Lily's attention. I've always thought she'd make an excellent spy. I may as well tell you the rest of it — or at least, the little I know. It seems that they found a letter signed by the German Chancellor and addressed to the King of Nepal."

"Do you know what was in the letter?"

"It's not hard to guess. Clearly, it was an attempt to enlist Nepal on the German side, against the British. England can ill afford to lose the Gurkhas, nor can we spare the six regiments Nepal has sent to India to free British troops for service overseas. Meanwhile, someone has been smuggling messages to the rajahs of the northern Indian kingdoms, encouraging them to rebel against British rule."

Sophie felt a sudden chill. "But that . . . "

"Could lead to a general uprising — to another Indian Mutiny? Indeed it could. And that's not something anyone wants to contemplate."

Surely, thought Sophie, such a thing could never be allowed to happen again. Troops rising against their officers, old grievances inflamed, old wounds revenged; innocent women and children slaughtered, the whole country in flames. But then she thought of the attacks happening even now in the streets of Calcutta, the veiled dinner table references to seized weapons and foiled conspiracies, and — still more frightening when she stopped to consider it — the news of mass desertions from the Indian army . . .

"There's no doubt," said Jeannie, "that this courier, whoever he was, was not acting alone."

"Which means there must be a German agent in our midst?"

"So it appears. I gather the courier is not answering questions. But Sir Charles is taking charge. It's not only Lily who has sources."

§ə

It came as no great surprise to Gangtok's small English community when Dr. Llewellyn was taken into custody. He was to be questioned by Sir Charles Bell about his involvement with the smuggled letter. There had been rising speculation that this odd little man was not what he seemed. Someone — Sophie assumed it was Sir Charles or his secretary — had contacted all the public schools in the English Midlands. None of them had a Dr. Llewellyn on their staff, or in fact had ever heard of him.

He was — it had eventually come to light — neither a doctor of philosophy, nor a teacher, nor even called Llewellyn. He was in fact Herr Otto Ludwig, German born but raised and educated in London. English speaking, English in appearance, but loyal to his German heritage, he had, one would have thought, the makings of an ideal undercover agent.

Why didn't I suspect him sooner? Sophie thought of his malicious attacks on Alexandra's reputation — clearly meant to deflect suspicion from himself. And there was the matter of the misidentified pheasant. Surely she should have recognized him then as an imposter. Compared to the devious characters in Mr. Kipling's novels, it occurred to Sophie, Dr. Llewellyn was a rather clumsy spy.

"What do you think will happen to him?" she asked Jeannie, who gave her a grim look.

"I imagine he'll be tried as an enemy agent . . . "

"And then?"

"He'll be shot, I expect."

"Oh dear," said Sophie. And had a troubling thought. "But what about the missionary ladies, Miss Ransome and Miss Elliot?"

"Entirely innocent of wrongdoing, it would seem. Quite taken in by Herr Ludwig's winning ways."

"In an odd way," said Sophie, "I feel sorry for him."

"Really? Why ever is that?"

"He really wasn't very good at spying, was he?"

"No," said Jeannie. "No, he certainly was not."

TWENTY-SIX

THE NIGHTMARES CAME MORE OFTEN now. Sometimes there was only a muddled and feverish sense of wrongness, of foreboding; though it disturbed her sleep, it left no clear memory behind. But there was one recurring image that made her so anxious and exhausted that she had come to dread sleep. Eventually she would plunge into unconsciousness, and the image would be waiting, sharper in detail than before and persisting long after she woke.

Was it a painting, a mask, a sculpture? It seemed to be a kind of demon face, part tiger, part gorgon, with long curving fangs, bulging eyes and outthrust tongue. In the dream its glaring shades of red and yellow hung disembodied against a wall of darkness. Surely, she thought, the image must contain some hidden meaning, some coded message she could recognize as a warning but was not able to decipher.

৯৯

On the day when everything changed, Sophie had awakened to a clear, bright autumn morning. Low hanging clouds opened up to a glittering view of sunlit peaks. After breakfast, her spirits lifting in the brisk air, she set out with Jeannie and

Alex to the market. Lily, in a splendid Sunday hat, had gone off to church, and after that to visit a friend.

Sophie had seen a Tibetan prayer rug she longed to buy. Woven in vivid shades of dark red and saffron yellow, it was very like one that belonged to Alexandra. But could she afford it on the modest allowance the English lawyers doled out from her inheritance? "If you're going to be pondering for a while, I'll leave you in charge of Alex," Jeannie said, and she went off to the spice merchant's booth to negotiate for supplies.

Sophie thought, *if only I were as clever at bargaining as Jeannie is.* The carpet seller seemed offended by Sophie's offers, and Alex was growing restless. Sighing, Sophie laid the rug down on the table and turned to speak to the child.

Alex was nowhere in sight.

"Alex?" And then more loudly, "Alex!" There was no answer. Sophie looked along the narrow alleyway with its jumble of tables and booths and kiosks. She called again, and felt a flicker of annoyance. Surely Alex knew better than to go off on her own. Had she gone to find her mother? Dodging around a pile of fruits and vegetables, she went in search of the spice merchant's booth.

Jeannie was waiting for her parcels to be wrapped. There was no sign of Alex.

Sophie fought down a rising anxiety. But what harm could come to Alex in this friendly crowd of shoppers? Something must have drawn her away in spite of all the warnings to stay close to adults. Jeannie, looking more than a little frightened, left her packages with the spice merchant and joined Sophie in the search. Separating, they went up and down the crowded lanes, past a blur of exotic jewelry, swords and daggers, prayer wheels, bone trumpets, carpets, curios, inquiring at every booth and table, using signs and gestures when spoken language failed, asking if anyone had seen an English child wandering about on her own.

Sophie could hear the question called out across the market in dozen different dialects. She might not understand the words, but she knew that all the messages were the same. *The little English girl is missing*

But none of the stall keepers had seen Alex, nor had the red-hatted lamas twirling their prayer wheels, nor the beggar woman crying out for alms, nor the sellers of trinkets spread out on green leaves on the paths to the market.

Sophie's throat clenched; there was a leaden weight in her chest. Jeannie came running towards her, looking hot and flustered as she pushed her way through the crowd.

"I expect she's just wandered off," said a young officer's wife — a pink cheeked English bride only recently arrived in Sikkim.

Sophie saw her own panic mirrored in Jeannie's eyes. Alex was a child of India. She knew its dangers. She did not wander off.

ॐ

All that afternoon and through the night, soldiers and police went from house to house, from shop to shop, searching every building, every open space, while others fanned out into the surrounding woodlands. They hoped to find some article of clothing — even a scrap of cloth, a hair clasp, a ribbon — any sign, however small, that a child, alone or in company, might have been that way. But there was nothing. Abruptly and incomprehensibly, Alex had vanished.

No one slept that night. Darius Mehta and Will Fitzgibbon joined Jeannie and Sophie in the search, and the Bells sent their household servants. Will seemed a very different person tonight; the jittery nervousness Sophie had observed on first meeting entirely vanished as he took charge of their search. Together they went through the village with electric torches, looking for hiding places where a child might have taken shelter from some real or imagined danger.

At dawn, after hours of fruitless searching, Jeannie and Sophie returned to the bungalow. Jeannie sat white-faced and silent. She seemed to have aged a decade overnight. Lily, inconsolable, was sobbing in the room she shared with Alex. The breakfast that the cook had set out on the dresser in the dining room sat untouched.

Sick with guilt and shivering from fatigue, unable to eat or rest, Sophie huddled in a chair by the unlit hearth. Her stomach was twisted into a hard knot, her shoulders ached with tension as she waited for the knock at the door she feared must soon come.

Her mind circled obsessively around a single thought. *It's all because of me, I am to blame. She was with me, and I looked away from her too long and took no care.* One momentary lapse of attention, and nothing would ever be the same.

At eight in the morning, the knock came. Sophie started and looked up, saw Jeannie's face go white, her body stiffen. Heart hammering, Sophie went to the door.

It was not as they had expected, a policeman, but a grim-faced Charles Bell. As she led him into the sitting room, Sophie heard the sharp intake of Jeannie's breath. She was on her feet, one hand grasping the arm of her chair as though to steady herself. "Charles — is there news?"

"There is, my dear. Not good news, I fear — but neither is it the worst. There is reason to hope. "

"To hope? Do you mean . . . ? Charles, is she injured?"

"No, no, there is no reason to believe she's been harmed. My dear Jeannie — it appears that Alex has been kidnapped."

Sophie's heart lurched. Sinking back into her chair, Jeannie stared at Sir Charles in shocked disbelief.

"Unlikely as it is," said Sir Charles, "I fear that's what has happened. And it's the prisoner, Otto Ludwig, who is responsible."

"But surely — he is in the guardhouse? He hasn't escaped?"

"No, there was no possibility of that. But it seems he has a confederate who spirited Alex from the market and is holding her hostage — where we don't yet know."

"How could that be? In daylight, in plain sight, in a busy market? Alex would have screamed, and struggled."

"We can only guess at how it was managed, but he must have been waiting for a window of opportunity. If Alex strayed out of your sight for a moment, that would be when she was seized."

But Alex didn't stray. It was my attention that strayed. How could Jeannie ever forgive her for that? How could she forgive herself?

"I say 'he,'" added Sir Charles, "but in fact we suspect it could have been a woman. In that crowd, an onlooker might assume she was a family servant responsible for the child."

"But this is insanity," said Jeannie. "Why would Otto Ludwig . . . " She broke off in mid-sentence, with a look of horrified comprehension.

"Exactly. Because he wants to strike a bargain. He has given us his terms — release him to Turkey, or to some Indian kingdom supporting the Germany cause. Then, he assures us, Alex will be safely returned to us."

"And you have no idea where he might be holding her?"

"He's being interrogated, as we speak. But all he's told us so far is that if the police or military attempt a rescue . . . "

Jeannie said bleakly, " . . . the hostage will be executed."

"Yes. But Jeannie," — he hesitated. "You understand of course — we can't allow this to set a precedent."

It was a moment before Sophie understood the import of those words. There was to be no negotiation. Sir Charles had no intention of agreeing to Otto Ludwig's terms.

Twenty-Seven

"M Y DEAR, YOU MUST KEEP up your strength at all costs," said Lady Bell to Jeannie, as she passed round cups of sugary tea in the drawing room of the British Residency. "And surely with so many people out searching . . . "

"But where to begin? "asked Jeannie. "There are just too many hiding places in these mountains." And turning to Sir Charles, "You suggested a woman might be involved. How well have you investigated those two women missionaries at Lachen?"

"The mission has already been searched, and the two ladies questioned. We've accepted their indignant denials. For the time being, at any rate."

"With respect, Sir Charles, I would question them again. Perhaps more closely."

This was a side of Jeannie that Sophie had never seen. A coldness, a stillness. A grimly resolute set of her mouth. If she found the kidnappers, Sophie thought, she would not hesitate for a second to kill them.

Lady Bell said, "But surely Alex must still be somewhere in Gangtok. How could they have spirited her away in broad daylight without being seen?"

"Think of how many merchants are coming and going, on horseback, and in bullock carts," said Sir Charles. "All of them with baskets and sacks full of merchandise — it would not be difficult to conceal a child."

Lady Bell was not satisfied. "But how would a stranger recognize Alex? There would have been other English children at the market. My dear, I hesitate to ask, but could it have been someone who saw Alex here at the Residence? Possibly one of our servants?"

"A day ago, I'd have said I trust my servants as I trust myself. But now . . . "

Sophie's stomach gave a sudden sick lurch. That day in the forest, Alex hatless with an orchid in her hair . . .

"He had a photo." Her throat was so tight that she could scarcely force the words out. "Sir Charles, it wasn't a servant. Herr Ludwig took a photo of Alex, and I didn't stop him." Her voice was shaking. Hot tears spilled down her cheeks. "Jeannie, I'm so sorry, I didn't tell you, I didn't think . . . "

There was a long silence. Then Jeannie reached across the tea table to take her hand. "Sophie, my dear, it's not your fault; you had no reason to suspect . . . "

But it is my fault. Sophie took the handkerchief that Lady Bell offered, and swiped awkwardly at her wet face. *From beginning to end it is all my fault. And there is no way that I can ever put it right.*

જ

A second night came, and still no news.

You must empty your mind of thought, Sophie imagined Alexandra saying. *Thought does not exist.* But there was no release in meditation, no rest for her exhausted mind. Near dawn, she lay down fully dressed on her unmade bed. She drifted into brief unconsciousness, only to wake almost at once with a dry throat and racing pulse.

Once again she had stood alone and unobserved in the shadows of a half-lit room. This time she could see crouched in a corner two vague, motionless shapes — a larger and a smaller; and glaring down at her in the flickering light of an oil-lamp, the demon-face that had come to inhabit her dreams.

In astral travel, Alexandra had said, *we can enter a zone where neither space nor time has meaning, so that we can move freely through both space and time.* But where had she travelled, in those fleeting moments? To the past, to the future? To some unknown place in the here and now?

She had to recapture the demon-image before it vanished from memory. She could hear Lily moving restlessly about in the room she shared with Alex. No one in this house would sleep tonight.

"Lily, can you find me Alex's coloured crayons? And a sheet of paper? Quickly, please."

Lily was in her dressing gown, hair loose on her shoulders, eyes red and swollen with weeping. She gave Sophie a puzzled look, but went to a bureau where Alex kept her art supplies. She handed Sophie a package of colours and a sketch pad.

With hasty pencil strokes, Sophie outlined the image as she remembered it: the skull shape of the face with its pendulous ears; the tear-drop shape of two huge eyes and a third smaller one in the middle of the forehead; the lips curled back from a mouth filled with enormous teeth and thrusting tongue. Then she opened the crayon box and began to fill in the colours — ebony black for the face, red and orange concentric circles for the eyes, more red and orange for the mouth, the teeth left white against the black of the gaping maw.

When she finished, it was almost sunrise. She found Jeannie alone in the sitting room with a shawl tucked around her shoulders. Lily or the housemaid had lit a fire. Jeannie glanced up as Sophie entered. "Still nothing," she said, before Sophie could ask the question.

"Have you slept at all? Or eaten anything?" Sophie asked.

Jeannie shook her head. "I lay down for a bit. I couldn't sleep." She gave Sophie a wan smile. "Cook brought me a plate of breakfast and I felt quite ill at the thought of it."

"Has anyone managed to get word to Tom?"

"Sir Charles reached some of the border posts by semaphore, and they've sent out runners — but he could be almost anywhere in those mountains."

"Jeannie, I need to show you something." Sophie held out the sketch pad. "Can you tell me what this is?"

Jeannie glanced down at the drawing. "A god, or a demon?" There was new flatness in her voice. "Himalayan, I think — but I don't recognize this particular one." She gave Sophie a puzzled look. "Why do you ask?"

"I saw it just now, in a dream. Or perhaps it was a vision. I no longer know the difference."

They stared at each other for a long moment. Jeannie had gone chalk-white, and Sophie knew they shared the same appalling thought: *What I see in my visions is death.*

"I'm in a room somewhere. I keep returning to that place, and each time I see it more clearly. Jeannie, it has to mean something."

Another woman might have asked questions, expressed doubt. All Jeannie said was "Sir Charles can tell us if such an image exists."

෨ઽ

At the British Residency, Lady Bell offered sustenance in the form of toasted muffins that no one bothered to eat. Called to the sitting room from his study at mid-morning, Sir Charles examined Sophie's sketch. He gave her a puzzled look." You drew this, Miss Pritchard?"

"Yes. From memory."

"Clearly it's a painting, or sculpture, of some tantric Buddhist demon. Probably Lepcha. But I'm sorry. I can't exactly place it." He handed it back to Sophie. "Is this something you've seen, Miss Pritchard? Has it something to do with the kidnapping?"

Sophie looked uncertainly at Jeannie. Jeannie said. "It's possible."

"Some kind of message?" Sir Charles put on his spectacles and peered more closely at the drawing, as though examining it for hidden code.

"Perhaps," said Jeannie, "but certainly nothing you'll find written there."

Sir Charles gave her a narrow look and seemed about to frame another question, but just then his secretary called him away with an urgent telegraph.

Walking back to the bungalow with Jeannie, Sophie said, "I don't think Sir Charles would have taken me seriously, if I'd told him about the dream."

"No," said Jeannie. "I suspect not. He may be a student of Buddhism, but he has little patience with what he calls 'supernatural claptrap'. What matters, Sophie, is that I take you very seriously indeed."

ℰℛ

Late that afternoon, a weary and disheveled Darius Mehta stopped by to report on the progress of the search. Sophie had left her drawing lying open on a table in the sitting room, and curious, he picked it up to examine it.

"Is this your work, Miss Pritchard?"

Sophie nodded.

"Gruesome looking fellow, isn't he? You've made him almost as frightening as the original."

Sophie stared at him.

"Oh, I take it this is from a book — you haven't seen the original? Well, it's a particularly unpleasant Lepcha mask."

Jeannie, who had just come into the room, said, "Darius — are you telling us that you've seen this mask?"

Darius looked faintly unsettled by the urgency in her voice. "Oh, yes. I can tell you exactly where it is."

Twenty-Eight

D ARIUS SAID, "THERE'S AN ABANDONED Lepcha monastery overlooking the Teesta. I took shelter there when I was doing field work along the river and got caught in a storm. "

"And you're quite sure this is the mask that you saw? "Pale and exhausted, her voice drained of emotion, Jeannie seemed to be holding herself in check by sheer force of will.

"Quite sure."

"We must tell Sir Charles . . . " Sophie started to say — and then, as she saw the look on Jeannie's face, she broke off in sickening realization. Sir Charles must not be told. The British government did not barter with spies and kidnappers. It sent soldiers with guns to enforce the power of the Raj, and what was Alex but one more pawn in their never-ending game?

"Darius," said Jeannie, "will you take me to this monastery?"

"You, Mrs. Grenville-Smith? You're not intending to go alone? With respect, you can't be serious."

"I'm entirely serious."

Darius hesitated. "Surely Sir Charles can find men who are specially trained . . . "

" . . . in covert rescue missions? I'm sure he could. And it would not be the first time that such a mission went badly awry. Ludwig will have given the order that at the first sight of a rescue party . . . she broke off, and Sophie saw her lips tremble as she fought to regain that steely self-control. "Darius, I'm not proposing that we undertake this on our own. Clearly, we need someone with military training. I'm going to ask for help from Lieutenant Fitzgibbon."

Sophie said "But he's a friend of the Bells. Won't he go straight to Sir Charles?"

"I'm prepared to gamble that he will not," replied Jeannie. "I think Will Fitzgibbon understands all too well how military operations can go wrong."

"I'm coming with you." The words were out of Sophie's mouth before she stopped to consider them.

"Certainly not," Jeannie said. "It's far too dangerous."

"I've been in danger before."

"We'll talk about it later," Jeannie said. It was the sort of thing she might have said to Alex. Clearly her thoughts were elsewhere.

৯৯

Lily was dispatched to the Residency with a sealed letter for Will Fitzgibbon. That evening a hastily convened gathering — Will, Darius, Jeannie, Sophie — met in Jeannie's sitting room.

Darius had brought a leather-bound notebook and referred to it from time to time as he outlined his plan.

"I propose, "Darius said, "that we set out tomorrow at midday — two English ladies on an afternoon's excursion, in the company of a family friend and a trusted native servant. Turbanned and bearded, I think I could make a passable Sikh bearer."

"*Two* English ladies?" interrupted Jeannie.

"I was given to understand," said Darius, looking flustered, "that Miss Pritchard would accompany us."

"You were given to understand nothing of the sort," said Jeannie, sending a sharp glance in Sophie's direction.

Sophie felt her lips trembling, and knew she was dangerously close to tears. "Please, Jeannie," she said, "I'll stay back where it's safe, I won't get in the way, but I couldn't bear to be left behind."

And from Will, who until now had said little: "Mrs. Grenville Smith, if you don't mind my offering an opinion — perhaps two English ladies on an excursion with a male friend would attract less attention than only one."

Jeannie gave him a wry smile. "Then I suppose I must bow to your judgment," she said. "But Will — your leg?"

"Much improved," Will told her. "And I can ride well enough."

"I'll see to hiring the ponies," Darius said. He made a notation in his book. "I remember seeing a rest house along our route. It's fallen into disrepair, but we could leave the ponies there, and it would do for shelter until dark. The rest of the way will be on foot, and we'll need electric torches." (He made another careful notation.) I hope you have a good head for heights, Mrs. Grenville-Smith. There's a cane bridge across the Teesta that has to be crossed, and I hope that it's still in decent repair."

"Mrs. Grenville-Smith," said Will Fitzgibbon, "do you keep a pistol?"

Jeannie nodded, surprising Sophie, who had never seen a weapon in the house.

"Could you use it if you had to?"

"Of course."

"And you, Miss Pritchard — Sophie. Do you shoot?"

"I have done," said Sophie, "at home on our estate." She did not add that she had shot nothing larger than a grouse, and had not enjoyed that very much.

"Then I'll find you a lady's pistol, and pray you will not have to use it."

୫ઽ

Jeannie and Sophie slept little that night, and they were up before sunrise, packing blankets and warm jackets and a supply of food. The day promised to be warm and clear. Well before noon they were ready and waiting, in long-sleeved cotton shirts, sun helmets and riding breeches. Darius had advised them to wind woolen bandages called puttees over their stockings and boots, from ankle to knee.

୫ઽ

All through the afternoon, they followed a narrow mule-track through a landscape that changed hour by hour with the steep rise and fall of the ground. In the heat of the day the forest seemed utterly silent and deserted; there was only the faint hum of insects, the crackle of branches under the ponies' hooves, the distant thunder of the river. From the flowering rainforest of magnolias and giant moss-covered oaks, the track led sharply upward, winding over dry, stony slopes, then plunged down a slippery zigzagging path through sal forest and bamboo thickets to the rank vegetation of a tropical gorge.

To pass the time, Darius told them about plans for the Indian Zoological Survey. He suggested they look out for rare butterflies and the small unusual creatures that inhabited these woods; but Sophie was barely listening, and neither, she guessed, was Jeannie. Once she would have been fascinated by this journey through a little known, exotic, world; now nothing mattered but the journey's end.

Riding behind Sophie through dripping undergrowth Will said quietly, "Miss Pritchard, if you'll permit me . . . " Sophie glanced round. "Don't be alarmed, but there are a number of leeches on your neck."

Sophie, who had felt nothing, choked back a shriek. Will rode up beside her and while their ponies stood patiently waiting he twisted several swollen maggot-like black blobs from the side of her neck and from under her shirt collar. As he scraped them off his fingers against a branch, he said "I'm afraid you have rather a lot of blood running down the back of your neck," and smiling, he gave her his handkerchief to wipe it off.

In late afternoon, they came to a low track that followed the near bank of the Teesta. There they found the derelict rest house Darius had remembered, and settled in to wait for nightfall.

While Darius and Will were feeding and watering and picking leeches from the ponies, Jeannie unpacked some sandwiches — though no one had much appetite.

"We should rest while we can," Jeannie said, and she spread a blanket so that she and Sophie could lie down. Presently Will and Darius came to sit by the doorway and they talked for a while in low voices.

Waiting for dark, Sophie lay on the hard floor of the rest station listening to the quiet breath of her companions, the rustling of leaves and scurryings and scuttlings in the undergrowth, the roar of the Teesta over the rocks. Was Alex awake, she wondered, and listening to those same night sounds? Was she lying terror-stricken in the darkness of her prison, believing that she had been abandoned by everyone who loved her?

If only she could reach out to Alex, mind to mind — comfort her and quiet her fears, tell her that help was close by, that she must be brave, be patient. She thought of the lamas who through intense concentration could send thought messages to one another across the mountains, like messages singing along telegraph wires. But perhaps that could only happen in the vast empty silence above the treeline; and in any case, (bemoaning her own shortcomings) Alexandra had said that psychic skill came only with spiritual perfection. And no one, thought Sophie sadly, was further from spiritual perfection than herself.

"Sophie, it's time." Sophie woke with a start to Jeannie's whisper, and realized that she had, for a few minutes at least, dozed off. She sat up, and looking through the empty doorway of the shelter, saw that the darkness had deepened. The waning moon was hidden by cloud cover and a ground mist was rising, though the heights remained clear and stars glittered over the dark towers of the distant peaks.

Sophie pulled on her boots, and felt something squishing under her heel. She took off the boot and looked into it with her electric torch. Somehow a leech had crept through the folds of her puttee, under her stocking and into the bottom of her boot and she had trodden on it. There was no time to clean out the mess; grimacing with disgust, she put her foot back into the boot and laced it up.

Leaving the ponies tied up at the shelter, they followed the track on foot by the light of the torches. They were moving steadily downhill, and the roar of the river was growing louder.

They had worked out a plan that seemed — they hoped — almost failsafe. Herr Ludwig had no reason to think that Alex's hiding place would be discovered; and surely, said Will, he would need no more than one or two guards — perhaps even only one woman — to keep a terrified child from escaping.

Will and Darius would make their way across the cane bridge under cover of darkness and climb to the monastery. Surprise was everything. Bursting through the entrance with pistols drawn, they would subdue Alex's captors, snatch Alex up and carry her back across the gorge to where Jeannie and Sophie waited with warm blankets.

For Will Fitzgibbon, trained in assault under heavy artillery fire against enemy lines, this mission, thought Sophie, must hold few terrors.

They came out onto a cliff overlooking a narrow part of the riverbed. Fifty or sixty feet below, the river surged over boulders between steep rock walls. Now they could see the dark mass of the monastery. It was perched on a spur of rock above the cliff on the opposite side. For a few moments as the moon slid out from behind cloud cover, they had their first clear view of the cane bridge by which they must cross the abyss.

"Good lord!" said Will Fitzgibbon.

There was a long silence. Then Will said, "It was supposed to be in good repair."

"It was," said Darius. "I crossed it quite safely. But," he added unhappily, "that was in the spring."

Two thick palm cane ropes were suspended across the gorge from cliff to cliff, the ends tied to trees on either side. Between these two parallel ropes, pieces of cane were fastened crosswise, and these in turn supported a line of bamboo poles that made a precarious footway. But even in this uncertain light they could see that where the bamboo should have been firmly lashed to the crosswise supports and tied end to end, it had in many places come undone. A careless misstep could mean a fatal plunge to the river below.

Will reached into his pack for an electric torch on which he had rigged a kind of hood made out of black paper so that the light could not easily be seen from above. He played the light along the first length of poles. Now Sophie could see that the poles were slick with a green slime, and more frightening still, there were places where the ropes themselves showed signs of rot.

Will said, "Is there another bridge — could we cross farther along and circle back?"

"It would mean at least two day's journey," Darius replied, "and we'd have to backtrack through some very difficult terrain."

Sophie met Jeannie's eyes, and she knew they shared the same chilling thought. Whoever had kidnapped Alex must have carried her across this bridge with little concern for her life.

Will raised his torch and peered farther along the footway. "I think I can manage it, if I go carefully. But it won't hold both of us, Darius. I'd best go alone. As soon as I'm safely across, you can follow."

"Better I should go first," said Darius. "I've been across this bridge before — though I admit it was in better repair."

"And how," Jeannie interrupted, "do you plan to bring Alex back across? You can't send her over alone, she'll be terrified. You'll have to take her by the hand, or carry her — and this collection of loose sticks and rotting rope will never bear that much weight. I'm lighter than either of you. I'll go."

But Jeannie was tall — almost as tall as Darius — and though she was slim still, she had a woman's figure, not a girl's. *Only one of us,* thought Sophie, *is slight enough and sure-footed enough to cross that bridge with Alex.*

She said "Give me a torch, Darius. I'll go."

"My dear Miss Pritchard, we can't possibly allow you . . . " That was Will, bound by his code of honour as an English gentleman — the same code that had given her a place in a lifeboat with the other women and children, while English gentlemen went bravely to their deaths. It was a debt that in an odd twist of fate she was about to repay.

Jeannie said with steel in her voice, "Don't be a fool, Will. Sophie's quite right, we have no choice. You go first, then Darius, and once you're safely across, Sophie will follow."

TWENTY-NINE

THE BRIDGE JOLTED AND LURCHED as Will stepped onto
it. He started cautiously forward. The narrow footway
rocked and swayed with his slightest movement.

Sophie watched him feel his way barefooted along the
slippery bamboo, his hands gripping the cables. *I mustn't
look,* she thought, *till he's safely over* — but it was impossible
to turn away. She wondered if Will was as fearful of heights as
she was.

As he neared the centre of the bridge, she saw it sag alarm-
ingly, the footway canting up under his weight in front and
behind him. He stopped for the space of a few breaths, then
went on, more slowly. Against all likelihood, the bridge held.

Jeannie let out a long shuddering breath as Will reached
the other side. He stepped off onto the cliff, turned and waved
to them once, then disappeared into the shadows of the trees.

Darius followed, his Lee Enfield rifle strapped across his
back. Twice he paused to crouch down, and Sophie guessed
that he was fastening some ties that had come undone while
Will was crossing.

Sophie was impatient for her turn to come, for the waiting
to be over. She could not bear the awful tightness in her chest,
the painful thudding of her heart against her ribs. But when

the time came, as it soon would, could she summon the courage and the will to step out over the abyss? She would be of no use to Alex if her nerves and her strength failed her, if she grew faint and giddy, as she had done in Kali's temple, in the Park Street cemetery, in the palace at Gangtok.

In the hands of the kidnappers, Alex would be frightened — but she would also be outraged, and obstinate, and argumentative. Suppose she'd been drugged, or hurt to make her obey, and was unable to walk, and Sophie had to carry her across the bridge? Or worst of all, suppose Sophie had been wrong? Suppose Alex was not there at all?

But now both Will and Darius were standing on the far cliff. Her turn had come. "Go, my brave girl," she heard Jeannie whisper.

And then she was on the bridge, the whole flimsy structure writhing and pitching and rolling with every step, and there was no turning back. As she clung one-handed to a cable and shone the torch downward to find her footing, she could see the black torrent rushing far beneath her and spume, silvered by moonlight, boiling over the rocks. *Breathe in, breathe out.* But fear was squeezing her chest like a tight band, making it hard to breathe at all.

For the first part of the way, she inched downward with the slope of the bridge, terrified of losing her footing on the slimy bamboo. But then as she approached the centre, the sagging footway rose steeply in front of her. An image flashed through her mind of passengers clinging in helpless panic to a ship's slanting deck as the stern thrust skyward. She forced that thought away, then sucked in her breath as a loose strip of bamboo tilted under her tread and one bare foot skidded sideways. The bridge gave a sudden jerk and shuddered beneath her. Nausea welled up in her throat.

Only a few more feet now. *Breathe in. Breathe out.* Now Will was grasping her outstretched hand and she was stepping onto the solid ground of the cliff top. "Bravo, Miss Pritchard," Will said. "Most admirably done!"

Teeth chattering from tension, she managed a shaky smile. And heard, from somewhere overhead, a frantic voice calling out her name.

She looked up. A bank of mist had briefly cleared, revealing the monastery gates on their rocky ledge — revealing as well a small figure scrambling down the steep slope below its walls.

A moment later, Alex flung herself into Sophie's arms, clutching her as though she never meant to let go. The terrible constriction in Sophie's chest loosened. But there was no time to ask questions, no time to comfort the child, no time to feel joy or simple relief. "Sophie, go now," Will was saying in an urgent whisper. "Take her back across the bridge while Darius and I stand guard."

"Alex," she said, "We have to cross the bridge. You have to stay close to me, and trust me, and not look down. Can you do that?"

From the face pressed hard against Sophie's shoulder came a muffled "Yes."

※

Alex walked just in front of Sophie, a hand on each cable, step by careful step. She did not try to look down into the gorge, as Sophie had done. But part way across, she turned her head to say, "I knew you were coming, Sophie."

"Alex, don't talk just now. You mustn't look round at me, just mind where you are setting your feet. Soon we'll be safely across, then you can tell us." The bridge seemed longer, the gorge more terrifying now that Alex's life lay entirely in Sophie's hands. Even now a careless misstep, a gust of wind, could plunge them into the dark water that seethed below.

But Alex was moving calmly, purposefully along their narrow pathway, and at last they were safely across, and Jeannie was at the cliff's edge holding out her arms. Alex said, "I knew you would come for me soon, Mummy. And Sophie too. And I thought if I could just reach you, if I could get away, so I waited till she was asleep."

"She?" said Jeannie.

"The woman they left to guard me. There was a man too, but he went away and left me alone with her. She wasn't unkind; she gave me a warm blanket and cooked rice over the fire, and gave me chai to drink, but I knew I had to get away. And I thought, what would Kim have done? So when she went outside for a minute I looked in her pouch and I found a little bottle of some strong-smelling stuff, and I thought that must be what she put on the cloth that she put over my face in the market so that I didn't remember anything until I woke up in the monastery, and I felt really sick and had to throw up."

"Ether," said Jeannie, looking murderous.

"And so I waited tonight till she was asleep , and I poured some on my handkerchief and put it over her face, and I found some rope and I tied her hands and feet together so she couldn't run after me." She finished, all in one breath — "I knew I had to hurry because the man who had gone away might come back, and Sophie, I knew you were close by."

"But how did you know?" Jeannie asked softly, stroking her daughter's tangled hair.

"Mummy, I just did. It was as though I could hear Sophie talking in my head, and I knew she couldn't be far away."

Sophie saw, and wondered at, the look that for a moment flickered across Jeannie's face.

Now Darius had safely arrived, and soon after that, Will reached the halfway point on the bridge. Even by moonlight, at this distance, Sophie could see his smile, and knew he must share her joy and her giddy sense of relief.

High up on the rocks above the monastery a dark-clad figure suddenly appeared. The man — if it was a man — stood poised there for an instant, seeming to stare down at the bridge, and beyond to the far edge of the gorge where they all stood waiting for Will. Moments later, he had scrambled down the scarp to the cliff's edge. With one hand he gripped a bridge cable. In the other hand he held a large-bladed knife. As Sophie shouted out a warning, Darius unstrapped his rifle, raised it and fired across the gorge. They saw the man glance up as the bullet whined past his head.

At Sophie's cry and the crack of Darius's rifle, Will had looked back. Letting go of one of the cables, he drew his Webley from its holster; but on that swaying footway he had little chance of striking his target.

Darius fired again; again the shot missed. The man with the knife bent to his task.

From the rock-strewn slope above the monastery there came a grinding, grating noise as though some ponderous weight was tearing itself loose from the earth. High up, a huge boulder was shuddering and rocking on its base. Warned, Sophie supposed, by its ominous rumbling, the man with the knife stepped back, but he was too late. The boulder, carrying with it a great mass of gravel and dust and scree, was already thundering down the scarp towards the cliff's edge.

Thirty

THE BOULDER GATHERED MOMENTUM AS it came. Narrowly missing the bridge, it hurtled over the cliff edge into the gorge, leaving in its wake a rubble of loose rock and earth and toppled trees.

The impact set the cane bridge swinging. Will, now past the halfway point, clutched the ropes as he struggled up the tilted footway. From a safe distance on the cliff top, Alex shouted encouragement. Moments later, Will stepped onto solid ground, and Sophie let out her breath in a long sigh of relief.

Now, as the dust cloud settled, they could see a woman emerging through the monastery gates. She came to stand motionless at the top of the staircase, staring down.

"She's looking for her friend," said Alex, and added with grim satisfaction, "Most probably he's dead."

"Perhaps," said Darius. "Or perhaps he got away in time."

But Alex was not content with that. "Mummy, you were watching. Do you think the boulder killed him?"

When there was no answer, Sophie looked round and saw Jeannie half-leaning, head down, against a tree trunk.

"Jeannie, what is it? Are you ill?"

Jeannie raised her head. Her face in the moonlight looked drawn and ill, and it seemed to Sophie there was a kind of absence, of disconnection, in her gaze. But then she straightened, shook her head as though in embarrassment, and managed a smile.

"It's nothing, Sophie, I'll be fine. Just a case of wobbly knees. It's odd, isn't it, that when the danger is over, your body betrays you."

And surely, thought Sophie, any mother, after all that had happened, would have that drained, exhausted look. All those nights without sleep, all those days of stomach-clenching anxiety . . . Now that everyone was safe, Sophie found her own strength and resolution fading. But Jeannie? Jeannie was a memsahib. She was made of sterner stuff. Something had happened on that cliff top that could not easily be explained; Jeannie, somehow, was a part of it.

Half-remembered remarks came back to Sophie now. What was it that Jeannie had said, that day in the Park Street cemetery? "Things have happened in my life too that I don't speak of, for fear of being thought mad."

But on the long journey back to Gangtok, Sophie tried to set those thoughts aside. She had been part of a great adventure, a secret mission from a Kipling novel. The mission had been accomplished with no lives lost (or one, perhaps, but happily not one of their own). The hostage was safely rescued. She, Sophie Pritchard, had acquitted herself well.

On one side rode Darius, the dark-eyed scholar with the face of an Indian prince, and on the other, fair-haired Will, the wounded hero. In Alex's favourite kind of story, Sophie would be the brave, adventurous heroine who by saving the day had earned their respect and admiration. Some surprises might wait for the denouement, but if you turned a few more pages all would be tidily resolved.

Sadly, in the world that Sophie knew, there were no storybook endings.

Thirty-One

A VAGUE ANXIETY STILL HAUNTED Sophie, but day by day it was fading. She saw too that the worry lines etched these past weeks across Jeannie's brow had all but disappeared.

Herr Ludwig had been sent to meet whatever fate the British authorities in India had in store for him. And now Tom and Thekong — thin, tired and windburnt — had returned from the Nepalese border. Before they had time to put away their gear, Alex was begging to hear about their adventures — "Haven't you had adventure enough of your own?" Tom wanted to know as he caught her up in his arms; and Thekong, beaming, presented her with a Blood Pheasant's red tail feather.

❦

Almost every month in Sikkim, it seemed, there was a festival. "Too many to remember," Thekong said — but he listed off for Alex the ones he recalled from his boyhood. In December was the Losoong festival, the Sikkimese New Year, when the native Bhutia and Lepcha people marked the end of the harvest season. In January, the Bhumchu ceremony predicted the fate of Sikkim for the coming year; after that was Losar, the Tibetan New Year ("masked devil dancers," said Alex, "be sure to write that down"). In spring came the grand pageant of the Saga Dawa in honour of the Lord Buddha when the monks marched with their holy scriptures around Gangtok. In the autumn festival of Dashain, the Hindu citizens of Gangtok smeared their foreheads with coloured rice and barley sprouts.

And now, hard on the heels of Dashain, came Tihaar, the five-day Hindu festival of lights that in Calcutta they had called Diwali. The air was pungent with the smell of firecrackers. The trees were hung with paper lanterns and lamps burned in every window. The fine autumn weather held. In honour of Tihaar — and to celebrate Alex's safe return — Lady Bell decided to hold a late season garden party in the grounds of the British Residency.

"May I have a new frock?" asked Alex, reading the invitation.

"We'll all have new frocks," said her mother.

"And hats," added Alex. "For you and Sophie."

"Garden party hats, I suppose," sighed Jeannie.

Alex's excitement was contagious. Lily, revealing unsuspected talents, set to work with ribbons and flowers and bits of lace to turn a pair of ordinary straw hats into elegant chapeaux. "And" (demonstrating) "you must tilt them to one side, so, for that is the new London style."

Lady Bell knew a clever Indian seamstress, and in the market they bought some lengths of silk for tunics and underskirts — russet and gold for Jeannie, rose and plum for Sophie. "Be sure to say the ankle must show, Memsahibs," said the fashion-conscious Lily. "My cousin writes that no one in London is wearing skirts to the floor." Alex's party frock was to be just like one she had admired in a magazine — embroidered white lawn with a green sash the colour of her eyes.

Dressed in her new finery, Sophie regarded herself in the long bedroom mirror. This was a Sophie of debutante balls and drawing rooms, of the world she was meant to inhabit before fate intervened. How little she resembled the travel-stained, dishevelled girl in breeches and topi who had ridden home from a great adventure. She wondered if perhaps she liked that other Sophie better.

૪ઈ

Lady Bell's guests included various officials and Residency staff, British officers stationed in Gangtok, and almost everyone in the small civilian English community. Through the sunny afternoon they wandered over the wide lawns and through the gardens and orchard of the Residency. The servants had built a makeshift bandstand, set out dozens of small tables and wicker chairs, and hung lanterns in the trees. A tea table under a marquee was laden with curry puffs, cucumber sandwiches, and iced cakes. Someone organized a croquet match, while the regimental band played Gilbert and Sullivan, and later a rousing rendition of "Soldiers of the King".

Towards evening, with clouds gathering and the ground mist rising, the party moved indoors. Everyone gathered in the drawing room, with its heavy old-fashioned English furniture and velvet drapes. The elderly aunt of Dr. Turner, the state physician, was persuaded to entertain. Accompanying herself on the piano, she sang the Kashmiri Song in a sweet, quavering soprano.

Pale hands I loved beside the Shalimar,
Where are you now? Who lies beneath your spell?

Then it was the turn of Mrs. Derbyshire, the major's wife:

On wings of song I'll bear thee
To that fair Asian Land
Where the broad wave of the Ganges
Flows on through a flowery strand . . .

Her husband the major was leafing through the sheet
music, and now, in a resonant baritone, vigorously accompanied by Dr. Turner's aunt, he gave them "My Old Shako"
and "Come into the Garden, Maud". Encouraged by the
applause he conferred with the pianist, who launched into the
opening bars of a familiar dirge. At the sound of those notes,
a chill ran down Sophie's spine. *Surely you won't! Not "Asleep*
in the Deep." I couldn't bear it.

Lady Bell and Jeannie were gazing with horror at the major.
In a rustle of taffeta Lady Bell moved swiftly to the piano and
whispered something in the pianist's ear. As Dr. Turner's aunt
segued expertly into "The Road to Mandalay" those who knew
Sophie's story gave a collective sigh of relief.

Presently Lily and Thekong came to collect Alex, who was
up long past her bedtime and overwrought by too much adult
attention. Tom and Jeannie decided to stay on. By midnight,
most of the guests had gone out to their waiting pony tongas;
but now some of the young officers, the subalterns, were rolling
back the carpet, and Will was cranking up the gramophone.

Will said, with an absurdly formal bow, "Sophie, do you
foxtrot?"

She shook her head.

"Then it's time you learned." And as a ragtime tune started
up, he proceeded to steer her skillfully around the room. How
much better Will seemed now, she thought, how much more
cheerful and at ease. She remembered all too well his shaking
hands, his absent, haunted look when they had met that first
day.

Breathless and laughing as the record came to an end, she asked "Was that wise, with a wounded leg?"

"Oh, the leg is entirely mended. Dr. Turner has pronounced me fit."

"Oh," she said. "Oh dear. Does that mean . . . ?"

"That I'll be returning to the front? That's for the medical board to decide when I get back to England, but I believe — I hope — that the answer will be yes. Fond as I am of Gangtok, I've no wish to sit out the rest of the war."

Sophie's mood had all at once turned sombre. She wanted to say, "But Will, you've done your part — why must you go back? "But no one asked that, not of a serving officer.

Darius had been an unobtrusive presence earlier in the evening. Will must have suggested inviting him, Sophie thought. When one of the subalterns put on a waltz tune Sophie looked round for Darius, hoping she could persuade him to dance. Never mind what the memsahibs might think — Sophie was English and in England you could dance with a friend. But Darius had already slipped away.

Will led Sophie out to join the last few couples on the floor. She liked the confident way he guided her through the steps; she liked, too, his hand firmly clasping hers and the warmth of his breath upon her cheek.

No one danced the old-fashioned Viennese waltzes now — the war with Germany had put an end to that. In fact, thought Sophie, the war had put an end to a great many things. But circling that stately Victorian room to a slow English waltz, it was as though they had drifted back to a gentler age. The drawing room windows were open to the autumn night and the air was filled with the scent of roses. All through the gardens, hundred of paper lanterns glimmered in the haze.

And now she saw that Jeannie and Tom had joined them on the floor. Tom held Jeannie close and they moved as one with unselfconscious grace. Sophie watched them wistfully. Her mother and father had danced like that, with the ease of long and loving companionship.

Will was smiling down at her as they glided and spun round the room, and there was no mistaking the admiration in his eyes. Her feet felt so light she might have been floating. *I am happy*, she thought. *This is what it is to be happy.*

From the slopes below the Residency came the *thwump, thwump* and then the deeper boom of fireworks. As the music ended, everyone moved to the windows to watch as the night sky lit up with shooting stars and fountains of fire and Catherine wheels.

Just outside in the garden there was a brilliant flash of light and a thunderous bang that rattled the window glass. Sophie jumped back in alarm.

"Was that lightning?" someone asked.

"No," said one of the subalterns. "Some fool down the hill has sent a rocket astray."

But when Will turned away from the window Sophie saw that he was shuddering as if the room had suddenly turned icy; all the colour had drained from his face.

She laid a hand on his arm, and quietly, as though nothing was amiss, she walked with him to a settee so that he could sit down. There was no need for him to tell her what was wrong. *He thought it was cannon-fire. He's not fit to go back. But if they let him, he will go back to the war regardless.*

Thirty-Two

O N THE OUTSKIRTS OF THE market a yogi sat heels on thighs, silently contemplating a tall bronze vase. A small crowd had gathered. Naked but for a loincloth, face half-hidden by his long black hair and flowing beard, he sat unmoving as a temple idol, scarcely seeming to breathe. Sophie and Jeannie were about to walk past, when a dull thudding came from the vase as though something was trapped inside.

"He's going to do some magic," said Alex, catching her mother's hand. "Mummy, please let's stay and watch."

The vase had begun to tilt on its base, first one way, then the other; almost imperceptibly at first, then faster and farther as the thudding grew louder, until finally the vase overbalanced and toppled to the ground. The watchers murmured among themselves, and losing interest, wandered off — all but Alex, who was clearly fascinated.

"Did you see, Sophie? He never touched the vase, not for a moment. How do you think he made it fall? Was there something inside, trying to get out?"

"Perhaps," said Sophie, as curious as Alex, and at a loss for an answer.

"It was magic," declared Alex.

"More likely a clever trick," said Jeannie. "Do please let's move on, Alex, I have to finish my shopping list." And Alex, quick to sense her mother's impatience, turned reluctantly away from the yogi and his mysterious vase.

But when Alex had gone to bed and Sophie was sitting with Jeannie by the fire, Sophie asked the question that had been in her mind all day. "Jeannie, the yogi we saw in the market, was that really just a conjuring trick?"

Jeannie put down her tea cup, set aside her newspaper. Though in recent weeks she had often seemed preoccupied, at this moment Sophie sensed she had her full attention.

Jeannie said, "It may well have been. I've seen far stranger things in India that were nothing but clever illusions." She paused as though waiting for Sophie's response, and when none came, she said, "You don't believe it was trickery."

"I might have once," said Sophie. "Now I know there are things that can't be so easily explained. I know that the human mind has powers we don't understand."

"Like the power to topple a vase . . . " Jeannie gave Sophie a long, considering look, and said quietly, "or topple a boulder from a mountainside."

Sophie drew in her breath. Those were the words that had waited unspoken in the awkward silence.

"Sophie, you knew, didn't you?"

Sophie met Jeannie's piercing green gaze. *Did I know?* Coincidences surely happen. It could have been a tremour of the earth that rocked the boulder from its base. What had she seen in Jeannie's face that night that could explain the inexplicable? She said, "I suppose in a way I must have. I sensed that some extraordinary thing had happened. But so much else was happening too, and afterwards — it was easier to think I had imagined your part in it. Yet all this time I've wondered . . . "

Jeannie reached across the tea table to clasp Sophie's hand in both of hers. It was an odd gesture for Jeannie, who was not usually so demonstrative. "But you didn't dare ask. Nor is it easy for me to talk about it."

"Does Tom know?"

"Of course. I've tried hard to keep it from Alex, but she has a way of working things out."

"And Alexandra knows." It was not a question.

"Alexandra has known since we first met. It was Alexandra who helped me to understand this peculiar ability of mine . . . this affliction."

"An affliction — is that how you see it, Jeannie?"

"For me it has been like a taint in the blood — a disease that you couldn't cure, that you could only try to hide from others, that you strove somehow to control."

Sophie thought how rarely Jeannie spoke of her past — of the years before she had married Tom. She had kept that part of her life as private as Sophie's life, in the aftermath of the *Titanic* disaster, had been made public. Now, as Jeannie began to talk of that time, Sophie saw in her eyes, in the deepening lines around her mouth, a remembered anguish.

"Imagine," Jeannie said, "that you were a girl of sixteen, and when you were angry or afraid, dishes leaped off the table and pots or pitchforks flew through the air of their own accord. In my village they thought me a witch. In Alexandra's books there are tales of sorcerers who can move objects with their minds, who battle one another in the mountains, and bury their enemies with landslides. And so I believed this strangeness, this power I had, must be a kind of sorcery. It made me ashamed, and it terrified me."

Sophie thought of Alexandra in her mountain eyrie, resplendent in her red lamina's robe and gold silk bonnet. *You must not fear your gift,* chérie. *You must explore it.* "Alexandra told me that any talent, not properly understood, is a torment to its owner."

Jeannie said, "There's a strangeness in Alexandra too, of a different sort than mine; perhaps that strangeness was what drew us together. For Alexandra the secrets of the human mind — and the secrets of the universe — are a source of endless fascination. But I wanted not to know what I might be capable of doing."

And you are capable of — what?

As though in answer to that unspoken question, Jeannie said, "Once when I was quite young — younger than you — I thought I had killed someone because I was afraid of what he meant to do to me. I hadn't killed him as it eventually turned out, but all the same, I might have done, and I tried never to use that power on human beings ever again. But more than once I've broken that promise to myself — and now, heaven help me, I may actually have killed someone."

"You can't be sure of that," Sophie said.

"I felt in my heart that I had."

"Only to save Will. You used it for good, not evil."

"Still, think how often bad results can spring from good intentions." Jeannie added with the ghost of a smile, "If you doubt that, ask Will about the war." She pushed aside her cooling, half-finished tea and got up from the table. "So, there it is, my dear. You have your answer."

One answer, Sophie thought. One piece in the puzzle that was Jeannie Grenville-Smith. But she sensed that there was still a great deal more to learn.

THIRTY-THREE

ON THE EVENING BEFORE HE was to leave for Siliguri
station to catch the Calcutta train, Will came round to
the bungalow. The family, gathered in the sitting room, said
their goodbyes — a tearful one, from Alex, and from Jeannie
and Tom a quiet Godspeed, with a hope for his safe return to
India when the war was over. And then Will and Sophie found
themselves alone.

"Sophie," Will started to say — and hesitated. Colour had
risen in his cheeks, and he was looking at her with an odd
intensity.

Sophie waited for him to go on. She realized she was
holding her breath.

" . . . Sophie," he finished, awkwardly, "do say that you'll
write. Please say we'll always be friends."

"Of course we will," answered Sophie, blinking back tears.
But was that really all that he had meant to tell her?

"Stay here," was what Sophie ached to say. *Will, you're not
ready, no matter what the doctors think."* But outwardly he
seemed so fit — his limp entirely gone, his hands steady, that
haunted look no longer so much in evidence. Was she the only
one who suspected how fragile that recovery was? But if he
stayed, he would be called a coward, handed a white feather

by some misguided memshahib, and for Will, that would be worse than death.

He took her hand and held it in both of his, and at his touch she felt a small shock, a faint thrill of electricity. He leaned down, and for a heart-stopping instant she thought he meant to kiss her on the lips. But instead he brushed his mouth against her cheek, gently, as a brother might.

"I'll write, "he said — and the depth of sorrow and regret she saw in his eyes seemed terribly like foreboding.

⁊ꙋ

Though in Gangtok marigolds and sunflowers were in full bloom, the late autumn weather was unsettled, with sunshine one day, and heavy rain the next. The high mountain paths where Tom and Thekong had done their research were snowbound now. Soon the heavy winter fogs would settle over southern Sikkim, making road travel dangerous.

On a mild, sunny morning, Sophie met Darius at the tennis court to play a final match before Darius returned to Calcutta and his work at the Indian Museum. The Grenville-Smiths were to follow a few days later.

Leaving the court, Sophie and Darius encountered Mrs. Derbyshire, the major's wife, who looked at the two of them askance.

Next day in the market, the major's memsahib drew Sophie aside with the look of one who steels herself to perform a distasteful task. "My dear," she said, "I really thought I should have a word with you. I know how difficult it must be for a young girl who has no mother to guide her . . . "

Sophie waited. She had already guessed what Mrs. Derbyshire was about to say.

"My dear, I hope you are being properly mindful of your reputation."

"My reputation, Mrs. Derbyshire?"

"Indeed. How to put this — I, and others as well, have noticed that you often go about in the company of the young Indian man who works with Dr. Grenville-Smith. I really feel it is my duty . . . "

Sophie had been raised to be polite to her elders no matter what the provocation, but this was too much to bear. The words slipped out unbidden. "Your duty, Mrs. Derbyshire, to tell me who I may choose for my friends?" She was appalled at what she had just said, but still, what satisfaction in Mrs. Derbyshire's startled expression and offended tone: "Miss Pritchard, there's no need to be impertinent."

"Thank you for your advice, Mrs. Derbyshire," Sophie said icily as she turned and walked away. No doubt at the next opportunity her rudeness would be reported to Jeannie or Tom.

The major's wife had reminded her of everything she hated about the Raj — its devotion to rules and conventions, its stuffy self-righteousness, its absolute conviction of superiority over anyone who wasn't English — or worse still, anyone who had dark skin. Darius had risked his life to save an English child, but would he be asked to an English dinner party, or invited for a gin and tonic at the Club? Most likely not. As she hurried to finish her shopping, her cheeks burned with indignation.

ॐ

On chilly autumn evenings by the fireside, the Grenville-Smith household read the *Times of India* and the English newspapers. Alex wept for the brave British nurse Edith Cavell, executed by a German firing squad for helping Allied soldiers escape from occupied Belgium. Jeannie waited anxiously for letters from her daughter Diana, who was nursing wounded soldiers at home in England while German zeppelins dropped bombs on London.

A letter from Diana had arrived in the day's post. "Not a word about the zeppelins," said Jeannie, "but she mentions that an old friend from Wiltshire is recovering on her ward. Do you remember David Cameron, Tom?"

"I do," said Tom. "He came for a weekend once. I think Diana was quite taken with him."

"It sounds as though she still is," said Jeannie, which prompted Alex to look up with interest. "Mummy, does Diana have a suitor?"

"Perhaps," said Jeannie, smiling.

"Do you think they'll get engaged?"

"I hardly think so," said Jeannie. "Not in the midst of a war. Diana says that David's wound is almost healed, and he'll soon be returning to the Wiltshire Regiment."

At Alex's bedtime, Sophie and Alex had been reading together from *The Jungle Book*. Tonight, though, Alex's mind seemed elsewhere. Laying aside the book, she asked, "Do you ever mean to marry, Sophie?"

Sophie laughed. "Some day, perhaps. When I am a good deal older."

"I think," said Alex, after giving this due consideration, "that you should marry Darius."

"Darius!" said Sophie, startled.

"He's very handsome, you said so yourself, Sophie. But he's also kind, and brave, and clever — and Mummy says those are the things you need to consider when you decide to marry someone."

"Oh Alex," cried Sophie. "I can't possibly marry Darius. Parsis only marry other Parsis."

Alex gave her a sly look. *And why do you know that?* the look clearly said. "Well, perhaps you could study to be a Parsi. Or Darius could join the Church of England."

"What a thought!" said Sophie, laughing. "And don't you dare suggest it to him!"

"Anyway," Alex said importantly, "*I* think people should be able to marry anyone they like."

In Alex's storybook world, perhaps. But so few of us, thought Sophie sadly, are free to choose the people we wish to spend our lives with. Tom, who was a baronet's son, had chosen to marry a poor schoolmaster's daughter, a common fieldworker. "And what a great fuss and to-do there was over that," Jeannie had once remarked. How much higher still, in India, were the myriad barriers of race and family and religious belief, of language and caste and wealth. "You cross those barriers at your own risk," Jeannie had said.

"But I thought we were going to read "Rikki-Tikki-Tavi" tonight." Sophie picked up the well-worn Kipling and turned to the tale of the valiant mongoose and his fight to the death with the cobra's wife. Rikki-Tikki-Tavi had won his battle. But in Sophie's own world, in the world of the Mrs. Derbyshires, there were even harder battles, ones that Sophie knew she could not win.

THIRTY-FOUR

F LAMES LEAPING INTO THE NIGHT sky, columns of black
smoke rising. blotting out the stars, the air rank and
choking. Burning in her nostrils, in her throat, a sharp,
sulphurous smell like fireworks.

*In the light of the flames, a gleam of dark metal. Parallel
lines of metal across a flat plain. Railway tracks. Along the
tracks, dark figures racing. The crumpled shapes of carriages,
overturned. And beside them bodies. Hundreds of bodies,
scattered beside the tracks like heaps of rags.*

Sophie sat up in bed, jolted out of the depths of sleep
by someone screaming. And realized that the voice she
heard — that high, terror-stricken, piercing sound — was her
own.

"Sophie, what in the world?" Jeannie ran into the room in
her nightdress, pulling a robe over her shoulders, with Lily
close behind.

"I'm sorry," Sophie gasped out. "I'm sorry," It was all she
could think of to say. Her mouth was parched, her forehead
wet with perspiration. "I was dreaming." *But in a dream, did
you smell smoke or gunpowder? The sweet, sickening odour of
burned flesh?*

Had she been witness to the past, the present? Or the future?

Jeannie said, "It must have been a nightmare. Would you like Lily to sit with you a bit? Or shall I?"

It was her mother Sophie needed. Like a child, she had cried out to her in the dark for comfort. But it was Jeannie who knelt in her nightclothes by the bed, and Lily, eyes wide with alarm, who hovered beside it.

"Please, can you both stay for a little? Sophie lay back on her pillow and found it was drenched with sweat, though the bedroom fire had long since burned down to embers.

And then she remembered. "Jeannie!" Her voice rising again, shrill with urgency.

"Sophie, what is it?"

"Tell Darius he mustn't take the train."

"But Sophie, Darius has already left. He had the chance of a lift to Siliguri station."

Thirty-Five

THOUGH IT WAS NOT YET midnight, Sophie could not fall asleep again. And in the morning Jeannie was standing in the bedroom doorway, white-faced, with a piece of paper in her hand.

"Sophie, I don't want to alarm you, but we've had a telegraph message from Siliguri. Last night a bomb exploded under the Calcutta train."

Sophie's stomach plunged. "Darius's train?"

"I fear it was. At least, it was the one he meant to take. But Sophie, that's all we know so far. Three carriages destroyed, a number of deaths and injuries. But whether Darius was in one of those carriages, we have no way of knowing. He may well have escaped."

Sophie felt as through her feet were set forever on a bridge of rotting cane, and each time she came to a place where the footing seemed secure, something threatened to topple her into the abyss. Her parents' death, Alex's kidnapping, now Darius — this time the warning of danger had been clear, but it had come too late.

౸ౚ

The waiting for news was worst of all for Alex. They could not keep the accident from her, and she refused to eat or leave her room until she knew that Darius was safe. Sophie found her huddled in a chair, face streaked with tears, clutching a book on Tibetan wildlife that Darius had loaned her.

Finally, towards evening, a second telegram came. There was a grim set to Tom's mouth as he opened it, but then with a sigh of relief he looked up and smiled. "Darius was in another carriage. He's shaken up, he says, but quite unscathed."

With a small joyful cry Alex threw herself into her father's arms. Sophie felt her own eyes sting with tears of relief.

※

"Jeannie, I saw the crash — I saw the explosion, and the aftermath. I saw the bodies by the tracks."

Jeannie gave her a startled look. "You were dreaming of the accident? Last night, when you cried out?"

"It wasn't a dream. I was there. I saw it happen. Just as I saw the place where Alex was hidden." She realized, as she spoke, how intently Jeannie was listening.

"Sophie, I want you to tell me exactly what you saw," Jeannie said.

Much like a kindly but persistent policeman questioning a witness, she led Sophie detail by grim detail through her vision of the train disaster: the column of black smoke, the flames, the stench of sulphur and charred flesh, the bodies flung from the toppled carriages like broken dolls. Sophie wondered why Jeannie, why anyone, would ask her to relive those horrors. When she had finished, when the last question had been answered, she was utterly drained and close to weeping.

Jeannie drew a long, slow breath. "Sophie, this is important. Was that what woke you, when we heard you call out?"

Sophie nodded.

"And that was at eleven o'clock, "said Jeannie. "I was still up, and I remember glancing at the clock."

"But the crash?" Though she had already guessed the answer.

Jeannie said, "We've been told, at about three a.m."

⅌ə

"Sophie, I've thought hard about what I'm going to tell you. I've debated whether I should tell you at all."

Her expression was sombre, and Sophie felt a shiver of anxiety. *What have I done?*

"I've asked myself," continued Jeannie, "if I have any right to involve you in things that should never have concerned you. But Sophie, what is happening in India is everyone's concern. No one is safe, we are all of us, English and Indian alike, caught up in terrible events. And in the work we must do, in the work that lies ahead, we need your help."

From that bewildering statement, one phrase leaped out at Sophie. "The work you must do?"

"Oh, Sophie, lass, surely by now you've guessed?"

And of course she *had* guessed. What had begun as a faint suspicion, a hint of unspoken secrets, conversations not meant to be overheard, covert meetings unexplained, had grown over the past months into what should have been certain knowledge. And yet she had been unwilling to accept that Jeannie Grenville-Smith — quiet-spoken, sensible, self-effacing Jeannie — could have a secret life as full of danger and intrigue as the heroines of novels. Still, this was a woman who had wrenched a boulder from its bed and hurled it down a mountainside, who once, by her own admission, had almost killed a man who meant to harm her.

Sophie said, "I guessed that what I glimpsed in your notebooks was not research for a novel. I wondered about the note that was passed to you that day in College Street. There were many things that made me wonder. But still I imagined . . . " She hesitated. "I thought it was Alexandra who was the spy."

With a look of amusement, Jeannie said, "If she were, I think she would prefer to be called an intelligence agent. But no — as far as I know — Alexandra is not a spy."

"But you?"

"Yes. A special agent of the British government. A spy, if you like. A cryptographer, to be precise."

"And Tom?"

Jeannie nodded. "As spying goes, it's mostly Tom. England, and India, need eyes and ears, even in places as remote as Sikkim. A zoologist engaged in a survey has reason to travel wherever he likes without arousing suspicion. And a zoologist's wife has every reason to follow her husband wherever he goes."

"And when Tom and Thekong were surveying on the Nepalese border?"

"They were looking for other German agents like Herr Ludwig who hoped to turn the King of Nepal against his British allies. Sophie, I'm going to tell you a number of things that you mustn't know."

"Mustn't know?"

"That is, no one must know that you know them. You do understand that?"

Sophie nodded.

"And you promise never to speak of them to anyone, no matter what?"

"Of course."

"You must remember that promise, Sophie. By showing you this, I'm breaking my oath under the Official Secrets Act. So then — "Jeannie handed her a sheet of paper. Sophie recognized Jeannie's small tidy handwriting.

A German officer, working undercover, has been arrested by the military authorities in Singapore. Among his papers was a map of Bengal. The coastline was marked with possible landing spots for ships carrying arms. Also hidden on his person, along with various compromising documents, was a secret code which allowed him to communicate directly with Berlin. He has since made a full confession, stating that he had been assigned to organize an insurrection against the British in Bengal, with Germany supplying both arms and money. He is to be referred to in intelligence reports as Agent X.

"Agent X," said Jeannie, "it sounds like something from a penny dreadful, doesn't it?

The security services are a bit short on imagination. But Agent X is very real, and very dangerous."

Sophie looked up from the paper. "Jeannie, what are you showing me?"

"A message from a British agent in India, sent to me for decoding. And now I'm going to tell you a lot of other things, and you must listen closely."

"But I'm not to *know* any of it."

Jeannie smiled. "Exactly. But all the same you must be aware of it."

Sophie had read her Kipling. She thought she understood.

Jeannie began: "For some time now we've known that secret cells in the hills and swamps east of Calcutta have been recruiting revolutionaries. Among them are expert bomb-makers who learned their knowledge of explosives in Europe. With the help of German agents they've been purchasing large quantities of weapons to be smuggled into India from neutral countries — from Thailand, the Dutch East Indies, the United States. Their plan was to spread unrest among the Indian troops at the Calcutta garrison, and induce them to murder their British officers."

"As they did in the Mutiny."

"Yes. And meanwhile the conspirators intended to isolate Calcutta by dynamiting railway bridges and cutting telegraph lines. They would seize control of Calcutta, and butcher the English inhabitants. Once that news spread across India, other Indian Army units would follow their lead, and the tribal areas on the northwest frontier, already a powder keg, would explode. The conflagration would spread across the country, until every trace of British rule was destroyed."

Old grievances inflamed, old wounds revenged; innocent women and children slaughtered, the whole country in flames. Sophie shivered in the warm room, her stomach tightening around a knot of fear. She said, "Alexandra believes that the end of British rule is inevitable."

"Alexandra the *révolutionnaire!*" said Jeannie. "But yes, Tom and I believe the same. India deserves her independence, and it has to come. But not, pray God, like this — in another bloodbath like the Indian Mutiny, with both Indians and British paying a horrible price. Conspiracies and uprisings are hardly new to India, but this one is masterminded from Berlin as part of the German war strategy. Don't imagine that the Kaiser is interested in Indian independence. More likely he plans to rule India himself. When the carnage is over, and the soil of India soaked in innocent blood, the Kaiser and the Sultan of Turkey will argue over what is left."

"Jeannie, I don't understand. You say you need my help. What part could I play in all this?"

"Do you remember that day in the hermitage, when you told Alexandra that you just wanted to be an ordinary girl?"

Sophie nodded. She was not likely to forget Alexandra's reply. "She said that I could never be commonplace — that I hadn't had a commonplace life."

"And she was right. Because she recognized this strange and wonderful talent you possess. I might have doubted her at first. Sometimes," she added with a rueful smile, "Alexandra's enthusiasms run away with her. But in this she was right. She saw your visions for what they were — neither dreams, nor hallucinations, but an actual witnessing of the past. Not only the past, it seems, but the hidden present. And now, beyond that," her green eyes gazed steadily into Sophie's, "events that have yet to take place."

Because I saw the aftermath of the bombing, Sophie thought. *I saw it last night in every awful detail — and I saw it hours before the crash was to happen.*

Jeannie said, "What government would not want such information? India needs my small talent for cryptography — but Sophie, how much more you have to offer!"

Power comes with foreknowledge, Alexandra had said. *Some outcomes are not random. There are some that will inevitably take place if nothing interferes with the logical progression of events.*

"But the letter said that Agent X has been captured. The conspiracy has been exposed."

"Exposed, yes. According to the Indian security services Agent X is cooperating and will be released, in return for leading us to his co-conspirators. Gun-running ships have been intercepted and their cargo seized. But Sophie, it's far from over. We have information that there are weapons and bombs still in the hands of the revolutionaries; there's still unrest among the Indian troops. We believe the revolutionaries are still determined on a major attack to distract the police and kill as many English as possible."

As many English as possible. When had Jeannie learned to state the unspeakable in that quiet, matter-of-fact voice?

Jeannie said, "I dearly wish that we could stay here, where it's still relatively safe, but we have duties and obligations in Calcutta. In a few days, we'll have no choice but to return. Something terrible is planned, Sophie. It will happen soon, and according to the best information we have, it will happen somewhere in Bengal. But when, and exactly where, we have no way of knowing."

Sophie thought of Will and all the young men like Will who had unquestioningly gone off to battle, eager to fight for their country and little imagining the cost. She understood well enough what the cost could be, in her own life, to do what Jeannie was asking. Still, how much less a sacrifice it seemed than the one that Will was making.

THIRTY-SIX

*S*OMETHING TERRIBLE IS PLANNED. BUT *where, and when?*
Sophie felt a clutch of panic each time they approached a
station. All through the two-day train journey to Calcutta she
half-consciously braced herself for a sudden jolt, a juddering of
the carriage, a thunderclap of gunfire that spelled disaster. Yet
there were no ominous dreams, no warning visions. Rocked
into a half-doze by the train's motion, she watched the vivid
green Bengal landscape flow past the window in soft yellow
autumn light. Paddies and wheat fields swept by, lakes filled
with hyacinths, mango and tamarind groves, white plumes of
kash grass flowering along the tracks, until she was thrust into
the clamour and confusion of Howrah Station.

৯৯

Christmas approached, but it was not like other Christmases
Sophie had known. A year ago she had been little more than a
tourist, fascinated by India's strangeness, only half-aware of its
dangers. Now those dangers were a part of her daily life. How
could so much have happened, in so short a space of time?

Once again the house on Park Street was decorated with
palm branches and poinsettias, the sitting-room mantel lined
with Christmas cards, the spicy scents of Mr. D'Souza's baking

wafting from the kitchen; but for Sophie and Alex, there were few holiday excursions. A year ago Calcutta's crowded streets had been dangerous for well-off Indian businessmen. Now everyone was in danger, Indian and English alike, and while the conspirators remained free, no street in the city could be thought safe.

Deprived of her usual pre-Christmas outings to the New Market and Flury's Confectionary, indignant at missing out on pantomimes and winter picnics at the zoo, Alex grew bored and restless. Jeannie tried to explain that the war made this year different, and Alex must try to be patient, for children in Europe were suffering far greater hardships than any she could imagine.

Meanwhile, Sophie pored over a map of Bengal, fixing in her mind's eye the location of the scattered towns. Might the conspirators strike at Siliguri, because it was a railway terminus? Darjeeling, because of its English population? No, she decided. Calcutta almost certainly would be the target. The British might have moved their Indian capital to Delhi, but Calcutta was still the City of Palaces, the enduring heart of the old Raj. Somewhere in that timeless zone where everything has happened and is happening, and is about to happen, a clue waited for Sophie to stumble upon it. But how was it possible that the lives of so many people depended on an ability she could neither control nor explain?

She turned again to meditation, to the chants and visualizations Alexandra had taught her, to the exercise of formless contemplation.

Imagine a garden. See all the different kinds of flowers, their colours and forms. See the trees, how high they are, how they are grouped together, the shapes of their branches, the patterns of their leaves. See in your mind's eye every detail of the garden.

Now watch the flowers lose their forms and colours, until they crumble into dust and vanish. See the leaves drop from the trees, the branches shorten, withdraw into the trunks, until the trees themselves are merely pencil strokes, and they too vanish. Then take the stones and soil from the ground, and make even the bare ground vanish. Now all idea of form, of matter, has been removed from the mind, and gradually one attains the sphere of boundless consciousness.

But through the long hours of meditation all that came was a nagging sense of wrongness, a vague unease that was like the perpetual miasma rising from the river marshes.

ℰⅈ

Sophie, reading in her bedroom, heard someone go to the front door. There was a murmur of conversation in the hall, then Alex's excited voice: "Major Bradley, I thought you were never coming to visit."

Sophie put down her book, smoothed her skirt and tidied her hair, then went to the sitting room to greet this unexpected visitor.

Major Bradley's ginger mustache was as fiercely waxed as ever. He was no longer leaning on a walking stick. "I had a sudden mind to invite myself to tea," he was telling Alex. "I've heard that your Mr. D'Souza makes the best currant scones this side of Simla." Then turning to Sophie, "Miss Pritchard, how well you look!"

Jeannie appeared from her office. "Major Bradley, how lovely to see you!" Though she was smiling and her tone was light, Sophie could see the tension in her face.

"Alex," said Jeannie, "will you run to the kitchen and tell them we have a guest for tea? And ask Lily to make you presentable. Major, do please sit down."

With Alex out of the room Jeannie asked simply and without preamble, "Is there news?"

The major nodded, with a discreet glance in Sophie's direction.

Jeannie had gone very pale. One hand gripped an arm of her chair. She said, "Whatever it is, Sophie must hear it too."

Sophie's heart began to race.

"It would seem," said the major, "that we can all breathe a little easier."

Jeannie leaned forward, her eyes widening. "Why? What has happened?"

"What has happened," said Major Bradley, "was a police raid earlier this morning that took over three hundred conspirators into custody."

So many? And as though aware of Sophie's startled thought, the major said, "There'll likely be more arrests once this lot has been interrogated. And I don't doubt there've been some innocents swept up with the guilty. But the conspiracy is broken."

All these past weeks Sophie's life had revolved around the imminence of disaster, her mind obsessed with a single daunting and improbable task. She had felt like an ill-prepared student facing an incomprehensible exam. Now, suddenly, she was told the test was cancelled. With that crushing weight abruptly lifted from her shoulders, life, with all its possibilities, could begin again. And she thought, *Alex will have her Christmas after all.*

৪৯

Nine days remained till Christmas. Alex's first wish, before the promised pantomime and Zoological Gardens picnic, had been to visit the museum. Today it was not the elephant skeletons she had come to see, but Darius. They found him in his cramped office at the end of a gallery in the Zoology Department.

"Miss Memsahib Sophie! And the little Memsahib! Do come in!" He swept some papers from the seats of his two wooden chairs so they could sit down.

"What a fright you gave us all!" said Sophie. "We were afraid we would never see you again."

"I cried and cried," said Alex solemnly.

"My dear Alex, I am so sorry to have worried you!"

"But it's all right now," said Alex, and added, graciously, "I forgive you."

Sophie asked, "Were you really quite unhurt?"

"I was deaf as a post for a bit when the bomb went off — but no real damage done. I had the very good luck to be in a carriage farther forward. I fear there were others who fared less well."

Darius took them to see the new exhibit of rare Indian butterflies, and told them about the preparations for the Zoological Survey of India, which was to officially begin next year.

"We must be off," Sophie said presently. "I promised Alex we'd go home the long way round, by the Maidan, so we could see the Christmas fair."

"Then if I may, I'll walk with you," said Darius. "I think the streets are not as safe as they once were for English ladies on their own."

Today the Maidan was gaudy with flags and streamers and scattered with white canvas booths. Sophie and Darius followed Alex as she darted in excitement from booth to booth, exploring the food and flower and bird-sellers' stalls, the fortune tellers' booths, the games of chance. There were costumed dancers, drummers and flute-players, a merry-go-round, a regimental band on the bandshell, a coconut throw. Best of all, at one end of the Maidan, there was a travelling circus with acrobats and tightrope walkers, and a patient old elephant giving rides to children.

"The village fetes we had at home in England were just like this," Sophie said. "Except for the elephant, of course."

Sophie was well aware of the curious, or openly disapproving, glances from the English ladies who crossed their path. What was in their minds as they observed this young Englishwoman and English child in the company of a young Indian man — an Indian in western dress, who quite clearly was not a servant? *Let them wonder*, Sophie decided. What they thought was not her concern.

They had come to the foot of the Ochterlony monument at the north end of the Maidan, a fluted Islamic column soaring over one hundred and fifty feet from its pseudo-Egyptian base and crowned by a Turkish dome. Darius asked Sophie if she had ever climbed the two hundred and eighteen steps of its spiral staircase to the top.

Before she could reply "Not yet," Alex interrupted: "I have. Papa took me" She added with a meaningful look, "It was quite exciting, Sophie. You can see all over the city."

"It sounds as though you'd like to go again," said Darius.

"Oh yes, please."

"If Memsahib Pritchard will agree to accompany us."

And Sophie, grateful after weeks indoors for the chance of a small adventure, echoed Alex — "Oh yes, please!"

Hot and out of breath, they emerged on a balcony at the top of the monument. Sophie had a moment of queasiness, seeing the gulf of air beneath her and the whole of the city spread so far below. But the floor was steady under her feet. She took a deep breath and held firmly to the rail.

"Calcutta is not one city but two," Tom had told her when she first arrived. She gazed down over the pale domes of Fort William, the English church spires wreathed with river mist, the stately public buildings of Dalhousie Square massed around their glittering pool, the broad green grassy spaces, the grand colonial houses in the leafy south. Nearer to hand, five huge cranes rose on their latticework legs over the still unfinished Victoria Monument, their booms etched against the sky.

And beyond, in the backstreets, beneath the untidy jumble of rooftops veiled by the smoky air, was that other Calcutta, with its many thousands of mysterious, unknowable lives.

She stole a glance at Darius's sharply defined, hawk-nosed profile. Alex's Prince of Persia. What did she know of Darius's life, of his Bombay childhood, his family? What did she know of his private thoughts, the life he led when he was not at work in the Museum? Perhaps he was engaged to be married, as Indian men of his age so often were. He too was mysterious, unknowable.

She took one last look before they turned to descend, her gaze travelling across the vivid green expanse of the Maidan, from the mazy back streets to the white marble edifices of the Raj. With the conspiracy crushed, the plotters arrested, her career as a spy was over before it had properly begun.

Yet why could she not dispel this lingering sense of unease?

Thirty-Seven

The Limes, Sussex

My Dear Sophie,
I trust you are well and safely returned to Calcutta. As you see, I'm at home in Sussex on a week's leave, and catching up on long-delayed correspondence.

You'll be interested to learn that while I was in London I ran into a sort of cousin of yours, Diana Grenville-Smith. We had a pleasant chat, as we seem to have quite a lot of friends in common. I gather that Diana and a Cambridge chum of mine, David Cameron, have what is called an "understanding." Of course any proper courtship will have to wait until the war's end. I only mention it because should a wedding eventually take place, I imagine the Calcutta Grenville-Smiths will return to England for the occasion. And Sophie, I hope you will be travelling with them.

There is nothing I would like more than to see you again. What an adventure we shared in Sikkim, and how extraordinarily brave you were! I've pictured you often, crossing that ghastly bridge, with no thought for your own safety. What a soldier you would have made!

I will try to write again from wherever I happen to find myself. Whether I am to return to the front is now up to the Medical Boards to determine, and that is to happen fairly soon. But I would love a letter from you, Sophie!

Your friend, and comrade in arms,
Will Fitzgibbon

Sophie read the letter through twice, then sat for a while with it open on her lap. Was it so wrong of her to hope that he would fail the Boards? How terrible to think of him returning a second time to the trenches!

She folded the letter carefully, returned it to its envelope and put it away in her bureau. Diana's news would keep for now. There was no point in giving Alex false expectations. But how extraordinary that Will should think *her* brave! Will, who without question had gone first across the bridge, not knowing if those rotten ropes would hold, or if he would plunge straight into the abyss. If he knew how close she had come to fainting from sheer terror every step of the way!

The Hermitage,
Above Lachen

Ma chère Jeanne (read Jeannie aloud, at the breakfast table)

I am hoping that this letter will make its way to Gangtok before the heavy snows fall and cut me off entirely from the outside world. The Gomchen has retired into his own cave like a snail into its shell (though I visit him often for butter tea and philosophical discussions). Save for my dear son Yongden and my two servants, I am alone in my mountain abode. Fortunately I was able to lay in my winter stores before snow closed the passes. From now until spring my diet must consist of barley flour, rice, turnips, lentils, beans — and at extortionate prices! They tell me this is because of the war.

As you can imagine, I have few amusements — though Alex would enjoy the young bear who comes by my cave every day to be fed. My rheumatism is troubling me a good deal, and I expect it will get worse as the winter advances. My dear Philip has sent me a warm robe from Paris, and that is a great comfort. As well, I plan to experiment with the Tibetan practice of tumo breathing. Those who master tumo can sit naked in winter on an icy mountain top, and by proper breathing and meditation, keep warm by summoning their inner fire. I will let you know how well I succeed.

Please give my fond love to Sophie. What a pleasant time it was, those weeks she spent with me ! I trust that she is continuing her meditative exercises. I see in her so much of myself, and of you as well, chère Jeanne. I feel she will come to achieve extraordinary things, though as we both know, it will be at a certain cost.

When this ill-conceived war is over and it is safe to travel again, I believe I would like to visit Japan. But first, against all odds and after so many discouragements, I intend to fulfill my lifelong dream. When summer comes, when the passes are open, Yongden and I will cross the forbidden border into Tibet.
Alexandra

Major Bradley was in Calcutta on another of his unannounced visits, and came to tea. As it so often did these days, the conversation turned to politics.

"I see," said Major Bradley, "that your Mrs. Besant is making quite a stir."

"*My* Mrs. Besant?" Jeannie looked at him with surprise.

"Didn't you know Annie Besant back in your London days, when you worked for Madame Blavatsky?"

"No. In fact, I never met the woman. I'd left Lansdowne Road before she and HPB became friends. But needless to say, I'm familiar with her reputation."

"I met her once or twice," said Tom. "Union organizer, radical feminist, rabble-rouser — a formidable woman. As formidable in her own way as Madame Blavatsky."

"Formidable, and potentially dangerous, " the major said, "Now that she's joined the National Congress and set her sights on Indian independence, we're needing to keep a close eye on her."

And just who, wondered Sophie, listening quietly from her corner by the fire, were *we?* She imagined a vast network of jovial, mustached, ruddy-cheeked Major Bradleys, sipping Earl Grey tea in parlours the length and breadth of India while keeping a keen eye on the doings of dangerous women like Annie Besant.

Thirty-Eight

IT WAS A GLIMPSE, NOTHING more, of a childhood terror — black shapes towering against a flame-filled sky. Even now those images, flashing briefly across her dream-scape, woke her with a dry throat and thudding heart. Something tugged at her memory, some reason why she found those shapes so frightening.

Next night the images returned and she saw them more clearly: enormous metal structures, like something built from a giant child's Meccano set, looming against a sky stained red by sunset. And now she recalled what had caused those long ago nightmares.

In the morning, she searched through Tom's bookshelves for a copy of *The War of the Worlds*. She opened it at the first chapter, flipped through the pages. Like all books bought in Calcutta, it smelled exotically of Indian spices. As a child she had read the novel secretly, beneath the covers. Nanny Perkins would never have approved of such an unsuitable book.

And here was the first description of Mr. Wells' colossal fighting machine, much as she remembered it: *A monstrous tripod, higher than many houses, striding over the young pine trees, and smashing them aside in its career; a walking engine of glittering metal, striding now across the heather; articulated ropes of steel dangling from it, and the clattering tumult of its passage mingling with the riot of the thunder.*

After reading that passage as a child she had dreamed of mechanical monsters stalking the earth on their enormous metal legs. But why, after so many years, had those all but forgotten fears come back to haunt her?

ℱᔕ

Again, on the third night, she dreamed of the metal monsters. Once again she saw towers of black smoke stained blood-red by the dying light. And now there was an acrid stench of burning, a clanging of bells, a rising din of voices.

She woke in the warm room with gooseflesh prickling her arms. It was an all too familiar landscape, that place beyond sleep where past and present and future co existed. Familiar, but no less terrifying.

Why now? The moment of foreknowledge, the vital clue to where and when disaster would strike — all those efforts were pointless now. Major Bradley had said that the conspiracy was crushed.

But surely this was a warning as imminent and as undeniable as her vision of the railway crash.

Suppose Major Bradley was wrong? A chill ran down her spine. Suppose there were conspirators who had escaped, plots that had never been discovered? However obscure the warning, lives might depend on decoding its message. She had a duty to report it.

ℱᔕ

"Jeannie, is Major Bradley . . . " Sophie hesitated, unsure what she wanted to ask.

Jeannie looked at her expectantly across the breakfast table. "Is Major Bradley . . . ?"

"Is he quite sure we're out of danger?"

"Dear Sophie, in India we're never out of danger. But if you mean this latest plot to overthrow the Raj, I believe he is. According to the best information, the conspirators have all been rounded up. Why do you ask?"

"Because . . . Jeannie, I've been having dreams — "

She had Jeannie's full attention now. "Just dreams?"

"Well, visions. But you'll think them very odd ones." And she described as well as she could the improbable spectres that visited her sleep.

"Are you quite sure they aren't just nightmares? We've all been under such a strain, bad dreams would hardly be surprising."

Sophie shook her head. "I've come to know the difference."

Jeannie put down the teapot with a sigh. "So you have. And of course I believe you. Never fear, I'll pass the information on. Though it's true — as warnings of disaster they don't make a lot of sense." She added with a wry smile, "Of all the threats we face in India, invaders from Mars would seem to be the most unlikely! Sophie, sometimes dreams are only dreams. Still," she added, "one learns to pay them attention. They can bring us answers, even if the clues are disguised as fantasy."

Thirty-Nine

A LEX — NO DOUBT ENCOURAGED BY Lily — thought that on Christmas Eve everyone should attend the midnight mass at St. Paul's Cathedral. "Too late and much too crowded," said her mother. To which Tom added, "Not even for God, King George and England will I stay up until one a.m." Lily, convent raised, looked discreetly shocked.

It occurred to Sophie that a large gathering of sahibs, memsahibs and British dignitaries, all crowded together in a candlelit space at midnight, was a tempting target for anyone bent on bringing down the Raj. More than likely Tom and Jeannie had the same thought.

In any event, the early evening carol service was grand enough to satisfy Alex's wish for pomp and ceremony, and her eye for fashion. Many of the men in the congregation were in uniform, their ladies splendidly turned out in fur stoles, feathered turbans or velvet and chiffon chapeaux, their silk-stockinged ankles discreetly revealed below their full-skirted frocks.

Sophie loved the gorgeous interior of the cathedral, its tall stained glass windows, its murals and Florentine frescoes, its plaques commemorating the heroes of long ago wars. She loved the familiar, unchanging order of the service (though how much more impressive here than in the parish church of her girlhood!). She loved the voices of the choir soaring to the roof-beams in joyful celebration. Even Alex, nestled sedately beside her on the carved wooden pew, seemed lulled into a kind of happy trance.

Still, thought Sophie, *I would like to come here when the church is hushed and empty.* Perhaps not to worship in the usual way, perhaps only to wander along the aisles like a tourist, examining the artwork without the distraction of other people; perhaps to meditate, or simply to open herself to the calm and quiet of the place. In the profound silence of the mountains, she, like Alexandra, had learned a stillness of the spirit. If only she could recapture that stillness, that silence, here.

ॐ

Alex was awake far too early on Christmas morning, eager to rouse the household. After breakfast there was a flurry of gift unwrapping (Diana had sent a box of books and games from London, and for Alex, from Major Bradley, there was a new Himalayan botanical guide with coloured illustration). Then came Mr. D'Souza's lavish Christmas lunch. The morning had been cool and damp but in the late afternoon the sky cleared and the sun came out. "It's much too nice to stay indoors," said Jeannie. "Shall we walk to the Maidan?"

Sophie was glad of the chance to go out. All morning she had been oddly wrought up and jittery, and now she felt too restless to spend the afternoon with a board game or a book.

The wide green sprawl of the Maidan was thronged with picnickers and families out for a stroll in the unexpected sunshine. A cricket match was in progress, and Sophie thought of Darius. How would he be celebrating the holidays with his family in Bombay? Everywhere she looked, too, there were soldiers from Fort William and officers in uniform, many of them with their wives and daughters. How pleasant it would be to have Will for company, came Sophie's wistful thought. Was he still in an English hospital, or — with the possibility came a sudden stab of dread — had the doctors decided he must go back to the war?

The cathedral was open all day to visitors, and Sophie thought, what better opportunity to explore it on her own? There was no one inside but a Hindu couple gazing at the famous west window with its Burne-Jones angels, aglow at this hour with the low light of the setting sun.

She wandered for a while along the aisles, admiring the nativity scene by the altar, reading the commemorative plaques, examining the frescoes and the intricate artwork on the eastern walls; she sat for a while in a pew, simply enjoying the dimness and silence. Then, realizing it would soon be dark and everyone would be waiting, she went quietly out the door and down the steps.

To the west the low winter sun was an amber ball in a sky the colour of fire. Sophie's gaze was drawn to the still unfinished Victoria memorial, where the stark black shapes of five construction cranes were etched against the sunset.

Those enormous cranes were so familiar a part of the Calcutta skyscape that as a rule she scarcely noticed them. But now . . . She stood for a long moment on the bottom step, staring at the latticed derricks, stolidly planted like giant legs in the midst of the construction site. Now suddenly, backlit by the flame-coloured sky, their presence was filled with a dreadful significance.

I dreamed of this; I dreamed of metal towers black against the sunset . . . And Jeannie's words returned to her with chilling clarity: *One learns to pay attention to dreams. They can bring us answers, even if the clues are disguised as fantasy.*

The warning had been clear, and she had failed to decode it.

Something terrible is going to happen.

What more likely symbol of the Raj, of the centuries of British rule and British injustice, than a memorial to the British Empress? What stronger statement than to reduce her monument to rubble?

She raced across the grass, and found Jeannie sitting alone at a table with a pot of tea.

Her heart gave a sick lurch. "*Jeannie, where are the others? Where is Alex?*"

Jeannie must have heard the shrill of panic in Sophie's voice. "It's fine," Jeannie said quickly. "She's with Lily and Thekong. They've gone to hear the band concert by the Victoria Memorial grounds."

FORTY

S HE HAD TO FIND ALEX, and Thekong, and Lily. She had to warn the people gathering at the bandstand. But who could she tell? Who was likely to listen?

They'll listen to Jeannie. Jeannie is a memsahib. She has authority. She'll find an officer . . .

Sophie was breathing too fast and her heart was racing. A sour burning rose in her throat.

But they'll ask Jeannie how she knew. They'll suspect she is part of the plot. They could arrest her. Jeannie is a spy and spies, even your own, are not to be trusted.

For a long moment she stood frozen, unable to act, unable to cry out, paralyzed by a terrible uncertainty. It was up to her to raise the alarm, whether or not anyone would listen. She had to make someone, anyone, understand — *something terrible is about to happen.*

Still she wavered, torn by indecision. Her legs felt rooted to the ground. Was it really to happen here, now, at this moment? Surely it could happen tomorrow, next week — or not at all. *And sometimes dreams are only dreams.* Who would listen to a girl of seventeen with a story of conspiracies and imminent disaster?

But there on the site of the Victoria Memorial was a message written in latticed iron on a sky the colour of blood. And if she hesitated — on Christmas day, at this celebration of a dead English queen, at a monument to England's fading glory, people were going to die.

She had failed Alex once before, and Alex could have died. It was that thought that sent her racing heedlessly, recklessly, across the grass, shouting a warning to Jeannie over her shoulder, that she could only hope Jeannie would hear and understand.

The bandstand had been set up on a grassy area just outside the Memorial site. As she drew nearer she could hear the band playing a lively march tune. In a long bank of flowers and low shrubbery that curved close to the bandstand, an Indian gardener was deadheading roses. In her haste she might have passed by without a glance, but every nerve in her body was thrumming like a plucked wire, every sense keenly alert. As she went by the rose garden, her scalp prickled with a feeling of wrongness. Perhaps it was nothing more than the gardener's watchful look as he paused with his pruning knife in his hand.

The regimental band had struck up "Soldiers of the Queen", and people were thronging close to the stage. Sophie strained to catch sight of Alex, or Lily, or Thekong. Alex would certainly have maneuvered her way to the front of the crowd for a better view, taking Lily and Thekong with her. But Sophie's view was blocked by a wall of dark jackets, blue and khaki uniforms, bright Sunday frocks.

"Excuse me, please excuse me, please let me through . . . " Heads turned to look at her with surprise or annoyance as she pushed her way towards the front.

On the bandstand, the soloist in his scarlet bandsman's tunic sang out in a robust baritone — the old words, because this was a celebration of Queen Victoria, not King George.

It's the soldiers of the Queen, my lads
Who've been, my lads, who've seen, my lads
In the fight for England's glory lads
When we've had to show them what we mean:
And when we say we've always won
And when they ask us how it's done
We'll proudly point to every one
Of England's soldiers of the Queen.

At last Sophie caught a glimpse of Lily and Thekong. They were standing off to one side of the bandstand where the crowd was thinner, each holding one of Alex's hands to keep her close. Sophie waved her hat, trying to catch their attention, but now the crowd had shifted, and there were too many heads in the way. "Let me through," she cried. "Please. I must get through!" Sensing her urgency, people stepped aside to clear a pathway.

As the song ended to enthusiastic applause, Sophie came up behind Thekong and seized him by the arm. He looked round at her in surprise.

"Miss Memsahib?"

"Thekong, take Alex and Lily. Now, quickly, as far away from here as you can."

The panic in her voice was all the explanation Thekong needed. "Little Memsahib, Lily, come."

When Alex opened her mouth to protest, Thekong silenced her with a stern look. Tightening his grasp on her hand, his other hand on Lily's shoulder, he guided them quickly and calmly through the crowd and across the lawn to what Sophie prayed was safety.

The band was playing another march tune.

"*Some talk of Alexander,* sang the baritone, "*some of Hercules,*

Of Hector and Lysander, and such great names as these.

But of all the world's great heroes, there's none that can compare.

With a tow, row, row, row, row, row, to the British Grenadiers."

The sun was low in the west now; dusk was settling across the Maidan.

For Sophie, the air seemed to hum with tension, with a dreadful imminence. But the people in the crowd were relaxed and high-spirited on this holiday evening, some tapping their feet and singing along with the chorus.

She turned to look over their heads, across the broad expanse of lawn that swept away into the gathering dark, and closer at hand, to the shadowy rose garden that curved around the bandstand. The gardener was gone.

And then she saw the small point of flame, the bright flicker in the long grass, moving from the near edge of the rose bed, from the place where the gardener had stood waiting for his signal. A lit fuse was advancing steadily toward the bandstand and the cheerful, unsuspecting crowd.

Something terrible is going to happen.

It was happening now.

The flame was racing through the grass. Sick with anticipation, Sophie fought down an overpowering urge to turn and run. Unbidden and unwelcome the thought came: *when the world erupts in flame, what do you feel in that first second — in that instant of time before there is nothing?*

Heart thudding, she raced up the steps at the side of the bandstand. The band, without missing a beat of "The British Grenadiers," regarded her with polite astonishment. The bandmaster turned his head to look down at her, eyebrows raised.

With all the authority she could manage, with the firm and confident voice of a memsahib, she said, "You must ask everyone to leave." And she drew his attention to the small flame in the dark grass, still some distance off but advancing steadily towards the bandstand.

The bandmaster lowered his baton, gestured to the musicians, and the music dwindled into silence. He turned to face the onlookers. "Ladies and gentleman," he said, "We have a situation here. I must ask you to clear the area, as quickly as possible."

Quickly, but with no sign of panic, the bandsmen gathered up their instruments while the audience began to disperse. Such situations, such sudden orders to clear an area, were a part of Calcutta life.

"Has someone got a knife?" The bandmaster's voice was calm but urgent. No one responded. Sophie, sick with anticipation as she watched the moving flame, thought, *if only someone was carrying a sword.*

The bassoonist said, "Will this do the trick?" and reaching into his instrument case he drew out what Sophie guessed was his reed-trimming knife.

"In a pinch," Sophie heard the bandmaster say as he seized the knife. He leaped down from the stand and seconds before the flame could make its way into the dark space beneath the bandstand, he severed the fuse.

Dizzy with relief, Sophie felt her legs give way. One of the drummers caught her arm and she leaned against him for support.

"Well done, Miss," she heard the drummer say. But she was uncomfortably aware that the bandmaster was giving her a deeply puzzled look.

FORTY-ONE

ALEX, BUTTER KNIFE IN HAND, gazed fondly at Sophie. "Sophie's a heroine, isn't she?"

Sophie, suddenly the focus of everyone's attention, felt the colour rising in her face

"Indeed she is," Tom said. He smiled at Sophie across the tea table. "As clever and brave as anyone in your storybooks."

Alex looked up from spreading mango preserve on her scone. "Daddy," she said reproachfully, "you know I'm too old for storybooks."

Is anyone that old? thought Sophie. But it was true, she realized with a small pang of regret. How had she not noticed? These past months while Sophie's attention was distracted, Alex had begun to leave childhood behind.

Alex said, "I knew Sophie was a heroine when she rescued me from the kidnappers, and carried me across the swinging bridge, and she wasn't a bit afraid." She paused for a mouthful of scone. Then: "But why was there a bomb under the bandstand?"

Tom and Jeannie exchanged glances. Tom said, "Alex, where did you hear about a bomb?"

"Lily told me. She said there was a bomb under the bandstand, and that's why Sophie told us to leave, and then she warned everyone, and the bandmaster stopped the bomb from going off, and everyone was saved."

"Oh dear," said Jeannie. Her tone was light, but Sophie could hear the tremour in her voice. "There's no keeping anything from Lily, is there?"

"But," persisted Alex, "why would someone put a bomb under the stand?"

"Alex," her mother said quietly, "there are people in this world — people like the kidnappers — who don't mind harming other people in order to get their way. And look, the teapot is empty. Would you run to the kitchen and ask them to send us another pot?"

With Alex out of earshot, Jeannie said fiercely, "I would like to live in a country where children don't know about bombs."

"There must be such a place," said Tom, and he reached out to put his hand over Jeannie's. That small gesture brought a lump to Sophie's throat. How often her father had done just that, when her mother was frazzled and upset.

Canada, Sophie thought. *There are no bombs in Canada.* Her parents had planned to travel there after visiting New York. How different her life could have been, had fate not sent her to this tinderbox of a country instead.

Like Alex, there were questions Sophie needed to ask. "But why *would* they want to blow up the bandstand? Not everyone there was English. Indian people would have died too."

"My dear Sophie," said Tom, "I need hardly remind you — their object is to spread terror. They're not particular who they kill. If this latest plot had succeeded as it was meant to — if the conspirators had seized control of Calcutta — it would not only be English blood that ran in the streets."

Sophie thought of the Indian businessman she had seen gunned down in the middle of a busy Calcutta street, and she thought of Darius, who could have died in that train explosion along with so many of his countrymen.

"But," she said, "I thought they meant to blow up the Victoria Memorial."

"Oh, indeed they did," Tom said. "That was certainly the intention. The symbolic blow against the Raj that would spark a revolution. The explosion under the bandstand was intended as a diversion, so they had time to lay their bombs in the Memorial site."

So it seemed that after all she had saved Queen Victoria's memorial, and perhaps for that she would be called a heroine. But how unimportant that seemed to her now. What was the Memorial but a vast perpetually unfinished marble cenotaph, a grandiose symbol of the Raj's power? What mattered was that she had saved Alex, and Lily, and Thekong, and all those innocent, unsuspecting people at the bandstand, English and Indian alike.

But a greater question remained. "The conspiracy, the insurrection — is it really over?"

The slight hesitation in Tom's voice did not escape her: "I think the immediate danger is over . . . "

"But Sophie," said Jeannie, finishing his sentence, "what you have to realize — with the world as it is, it's never, ever, really over."

❧

Those words of Jeannie's, hovering between despair and resignation, came back to Sophie a few days later upon the arrival of a letter from Sikkim. When Jeannie opened the envelope at the breakfast table, her sombre look warned Sophie that it brought unwelcome news.

"It's from Lady Bell," Jeannie said, when she had scanned the page, "and Sophie, I'm afraid the message is meant for you as well."

I'm so sorry to say that we have had distressing news from the War Office about Charles' young relative Will Fitzgibbon. Will wrote to us from England that he was likely to be declared fit by the Medical Boards and would be returning to active service. Now, sadly, we have heard from the War Office that he has gone missing in action. Charles believes that he was serving somewhere in northern France, but needless to say, they never give you the exact location.

I thought that you and Tom, and Sophie and Alex as well, would want to know. Will of course was such a help to your family in Sikkim, and he has told me how very fond he was of your lovely Sophie.

I will certainly write again at once if we have further news.

Will *had* been fond of her. She had read that in his eyes, in the warmth of his smile, all those months ago in Sikkim. She had read it more clearly still in the letter he had sent from Sussex.

She thought of Will's gallantry, his courage, the generosity of his undemanding friendship. She thought of his wry self-effacing smile, and the cornflower colour of his eyes. She must not for a moment think of him lying dead in France in a waste of blood-soaked mud. But that was the image she could not shut out.

She had known that he was not fit to return to the war, might never be fit, no matter what the doctors and the generals said. But what was her small voice, against the ponderous weight of military honour?

So she had said nothing, and the chance to save him, slight though it might have been, was lost. Will had been fond of her, and she had been fond of Will. Fonder than she had understood until this moment as she fled from the table sick with grief and regret.

Forty-Two

I N HER DREAM, SHE SAW a figure moving through a dark coniferous forest. It seemed to be evening, or just before dawn. Shadows lay heavy on the ground; the treetops appeared to float in mist. The figure — she guessed by his height and his clothing that it was a man — walked slowly, and she imagined that he was limping.

She could not see his face. He could have been anyone at all — a stranger lost and injured in a forest anywhere on earth. Yet in that first moment after waking she let herself imagine it could be Will.

She knew that when a letter came to say a soldier was not dead but missing, it offered no hopeful message. It meant only that his body could not be found. The missing returned only in dreams, as shadows created from desperate hope and grief, and longing.

ॐ

Sophie and Jeannie had been kept waiting on hard wooden chairs for the last half hour. The room was drab and institutional. There was a large oak desk with stacks of papers, some wooden filing cabinets. The king's picture hung on the beige wall behind the desk. The air smelled of cigarettes and floor wax.

Why on earth were they here? Why had Sophie been summoned by letter to this bleak office in a backstreet off the Chowringhee Road? Jeannie, who had accompanied her, had no answer. At first Sophie had wondered if they — whoever *they* might be — intended to thank her for her part in saving the Victoria Memorial. But no, she thought, when she saw the unsmiling face of the man who eventually entered the room and sat down in the chair behind the desk. He was not a British army officer as she had expected, nor a member of the Indian Police. He was clearly British, but in civilian clothes, and when his cold grey eyes stared at Sophie across the cluttered desk, she felt like a pupil called before the headmaster to explain some foolhardy prank.

He introduced himself as Inspector Grey. "And you are Miss Sophie Pritchard?"

Sophie nodded. And she knew with a shock of understanding, *this is an interrogation.*

"And you are the ward of Dr. and Mrs. Grenville-Smith?"

Their ward? Is that what I am? She glanced nervously at Jeannie, who nodded.

"Yes. That is — they've been kind enough to take me into their family."

"Miss Pritchard, I've asked you to come in today, because there is a small matter in need of clearing up. I understand you're the young woman who raised the alarm about the bomb in the Victoria Memorial grounds?"

"Yes."

"And needless to say we are all very grateful that you did so. But one thing puzzles me, Miss Pritchard. No one else it seems was aware of that bomb planted under the bandstand.

How was it you knew it was there, and were able to call out a warning?"

"Because — " How on earth could she explain? "Because I had a sense that something was wrong."

"A sense, Miss Pritchard? What do you mean? Some sort of premonition?"

Jeannie caught Sophie's eye. *Go carefully*, that glance said.

"Not a premonition, exactly... Just the sense one sometimes has — the feeling that things are not quite right."

"Can you be more specific?"

She thought quickly. "There was a gardener near the bandstand, just waiting, not working, with a sort of watchful look. That seemed odd to me."

"I see," said Inspector Grey.

"Oh — and then I noticed the burning fuse, and so I was sure."

"The fuse in the grass, that no one else noticed."

"Yes — but they were all looking towards the band, and the singer."

"Everyone but you, it appears."

"Yes."

"Very well, Miss Pritchard. I just have one more question. A few days ago you were seen walking on the Maidan with a young Indian man — not, I gather, a family servant. Would you mind telling me who he was?"

Indeed I do mind, Sophie thought indignantly. But Inspector Grey — whoever *he* was — was waiting for an answer.

"A friend," she said — and Jeannie finished for her: "A family friend. He's a research assistant who works with my husband."

"His name, if you please?" said the inspector.

"Darius," said Sophie, half in a whisper. "Darius Mehta." And she thought, *what have I done?*

"Thank you. Miss Pritchard, Mrs. Grenville-Smith. You may go — though I may have more questions later."

ᡈᢒ

"Jeannie, what should I have said? I couldn't tell him how I knew about the bomb."

"No," Jeannie said. "And he wouldn't have believed it. He'd simply have thought you were lying — and he would want to know why."

"But do you know who he is?"

"Counter-intelligence, I assume. Probably Special Branch. Certainly no one I know. Nor was I aware of this building. And Sophie, I'm so sorry — I knew there'd have to be questions, but I had no idea you would be drawn into it like this. You were put in an impossible position, and you did the very best you could."

"But Darius? Why did he want to know about Darius?"

Jeannie shook her head. "I have absolutely no idea. But Sophie, I'm sorry to say this — I expect we'll find out soon enough."

FORTY-THREE

THE YEAR TURNED. EARLY 1916 brought the British army heavy losses on the Western Front and in the war against the Turks in Mesopotamia. In January, Britain introduced military conscription, and in January too, in a year holding little promise of an end to turmoil, came Sophie's eighteenth birthday.

Jeannie and Tom gave her a Tibetan necklace of silver and turquoise, and Alex presented her with a collection of carefully pressed and dried Himalayan wildflowers, each one marked with its Latin name and the location where it had been found. In honour of the occasion, their cook Mr. D'Souza baked a Battenberg cake for tea.

A day later, Sophie's world was once again turned upside down.

Tom arrived home from the museum in mid-afternoon with his usually cheerful face set in grim lines. "Where is Alex at the moment?" he asked as the front door closed behind him.

"In the garden with Lily," Jeannie told him. "Tom, why?"

"Because I have some disturbing news, that I'd rather Alex not hear." He turned to Sophie. "My dear, I know this will distress you, as much as it has me. Apparently Darius has been arrested."

Sophie heard Jeannie's small gasp, and her own heart gave a sickening lurch. She thought at once of stories she had heard, of how the police treated their Indian prisoners.

"Surely not," said Jeannie. "On what grounds?"

Tom said, "I only have this second-hand, but they're suspecting him of involvement in the Christmas bomb attempt."

With horror, Sophie realized what must be happening, what misguided and terrible connections had been made. And by whom? The police? Special Branch? Indian Intelligence Bureau? By the mysterious Mr. Grey in his carefully anonymous office?

She had only the vaguest idea of the tangled webs of spy and anti-terrorist agencies that existed under the Raj — but surely it was in one of those that Darius had been trapped.

She knew that as an English girl, not yet twenty-one and still new to India, she was herself an unlikely suspect. But clearly, she had prior knowledge of the bomb plot. How else could she have known to cry out a warning? She had been seen in the company of a young Indian man. And every young Indian man in these turbulent times — especially one university trained — was a likely suspect. What secret plans might he have revealed to Sophie, if only accidentally?

"But they will beat him," she said. Her lips were trembling. "He's done nothing, and they will beat him."

Tom and Jeannie exchanged a glance. That brief look told Sophie far more than she wished to know.

Forty-Four

A male clerk met them in the outer office. "Mrs. Grenville-Smith, the Inspector would like to speak to Miss Pritchard alone."

"I can't allow that," Jeannie said. "Miss Pritchard is a minor, under my protection. Tell the Inspector if he needs to question her, it has to be in my presence."

Faced with this determined memsahib, the young clerk looked flustered. "But I must insist . . . "

"And so must I," said Jeannie. "You will please tell the Inspector . . . "

Sophie stood up, smoothed down her skirt, put up a hand to straighten her hair. "Jeannie, it's all right. I don't mind. I'll talk to him. You'll wait for me here?"

"Yes, of course, but Sophie . . . "

"I'm eighteen," said Sophie. "I'm not a child any more, Jeannie. I'm able to do this."

"Miss Pritchard, I've asked you back today, because I have a few more questions."

Sophie waited. Her chest was so tight with tension it was hard to breathe.

The Inspector made a show of shuffling some papers on his desk. "In examining our files we have come across some interesting connections. Miss Pritchard, I believe you are familiar with the name Alexandra David Neel?"

Alexandra? Sophie gave a start of surprise. What had Alexandra, in her mountain hideaway, to do with any of this? But the inspector, steely-eyed and impassive, was waiting for an answer. "Yes, of course," she said.

"And you are aware that she is a close friend of Mrs. Grenville-Smith? That in fact they have known each other since their youth?"

Why is he asking me this?

"You are aware of that, Miss Pritchard?"

Sophie nodded.

"Answer aloud, if you please."

"Yes. I believe so."

"And were you aware that in Paris Madame David-Neel associated with known anarchists — was in all probability herself an anarchist?"

Sophie's stomach twisted. Nausea rose in her throat. *It's not enough to accuse Darius. He's drawing Alexandra into this. And Jeannie is Alexandra's friend.*

When Sophie remained silent, the Inspector gave her a narrow look. "You prefer not to reply? Then I must assume the answer is yes. So, Miss Pritchard. One more question and you can go."

Sophie waited, holding her breath.

"Are you familiar with the name Mrs. Annie Besant?"

"No," she started to say. Then she remembered. Tea with Major Bradley, the conversation turning to Indian politics, and the demands for home rule. A rabble rouser, Tom had called Annie Besant. A potentially dangerous woman, the major had said.

"I may have heard her name mentioned."

"I'm sure you have, Miss Pritchard. "Her name is all over the newspapers, with her plan for a Home Rule League. If you tell me you don't know the woman, then I say you are being less than truthful."

Suddenly she was angry. No longer frightened and indignant but seized by a rage that made her heart pound in her rib cage, her face grow hot and flushed.

"Inspector Grey. I don't lie. My parents taught me at all costs to tell the truth. So I am telling the truth when I say that whatever absurd conspiracies you may have imagined — or *invented* — there is no substance to any of them."

She knew her voice was rising, growing shrill, and she struggled to control it. She must speak coolly and deliberately. She must sound as serenely self-confident as Jeannie did in her haughtiest memsahib moments.

She said, "Jean Grenville-Smith is a woman of impeccable reputation. To suggest that she has anarchist connections is insulting and ridiculous, and whatever you may have against Mrs. Besant, she has never been an associate of Mrs. Grenville-Smith's. In fact, the two have never met."

She was running out of breath; her heart went on thudding painfully in her chest, and she could feel her voice growing hoarse and scratchy. But she had to finish. "And Darius Mehta? He is a brave, loyal friend, and a scholar. I doubt that he has much interest in politics, let alone any involvement."

"And you assure me, Miss Pritchard, that neither he nor you had previous knowledge of this plot to bomb the monument? You're asking me to believe that you based your warning on some sort of intuition?"

"Yes," she said. "As I have already told you . . . "

"Yes. So you did. The gardener, and the fuse no one else saw. And have you had these . . . *inklings* . . . on other occasions?"

She hesitated, torn for a dreadful moment between her need to save Darius, and her fear of what official secrets she might reveal.

"Yes," she said. "Sometimes. As one does."

"I see," said the inspector, who by his expression clearly did not see at all. "Does one, indeed? Then if I asked you to tell me which batsman is going to score the most runs in next Sunday's test match, you could tell me?"

"Of course I couldn't."

"Then Miss Pritchard, I find it difficult to believe you did not obtain the information in some more conventional way."

She had tried for so long to smother her anger at the pride and arrogance and casual injustices of the Raj. And now to face the accusations of this cold eyed, mean spirited little man . . .

"You have it all wrong, Inspector. This web you are trying to spin — and I can't imagine your reason — there is not a thread of truth in any of it."

And then, appalled at what she was about to say, even before the words were out: "My father when he was alive was a cabinet minister, and my mother was the daughter of a Viscount. When I discover who your superiors are, I mean to report you as a liar and a bully."

Inspector Smith had the look (as Sophie was to remember later) of a stoat unexpectedly bitten by the rabbit he had meant to seize in his jaws.

❀

Only when she was back in familiar surroundings did Sophie realize the depth of her exhaustion. She felt as drained as if she were recovering from an illness. Tom, seeing her shiver, stirred up the sitting room fire.

"You were very brave," he told her, "to face that interrogation alone."

"Oh, Tom," she said, "I was not brave at all. And I did something really foolish."

Tom set down his Scotch whisky and water and regarded her with raised brows.

"I told him that my father was a cabinet minister and my mother was a Viscount's daughter. I said I would report him to his superiors. Was that awful of me, Tom?"

"Not a bit of it," said Tom. "Men like him are easily cowed by titles, and when you have to deal with them, you use whatever weapons you have at hand. I dare say Inspector Smith looked you up in Debrett's Guide to the Peerage and found your father in the parliamentary records, and when he saw you were telling the truth, he asked himself how many important people he had managed to offend."

"But Tom, couldn't I be charged under the Defense of India Act?"

"My dear child, for what?"

"I threatened an agent of the Raj. "

Tom laughed. "Your agent of the Raj is a little man, Sophie, of no importance, with ambitions beyond his abilities, and he's concocted this conspiracy theory in the hope of promotion. I think you have thoroughly routed him."

"But what of Darius? He's still in prison."

"But not for long. There was never any real evidence against him — he was merely the first link in Inspector Smith's confabulations. Now Smith will back down, and Darius will be released. He has you to thank for that, Sophie."

"But I was the one who involved him in all this. I was the first link in the chain."

"Which, from what you've told us," said Jeannie, "went on to involve me, and Alexandra, and probably Tom, and — heaven help us — Annie Besant. So we all of us thank you, Sophie Pritchard, for standing up to the bully. You've saved us a good deal of embarrassment."

FORTY-FIVE

S OPHIE GUESSED THAT THIS EVENING was a celebration of Darius's release from prison.

Mr. D'Souza had outdone himself with his famous fish curry, the table was laid with Jeannie's best china, and for pudding there was an elaborate trifle. Here, gathered with Sophie in the lamp-lit dining room, were the five people who inhabited the centre of her world. At her left elbow was Tom, still darkly tanned from a summer in the hills. Major Bradley was on her right, and when she turned to speak to him, she saw that over the past year grey threads had crept into his ginger moustache. Here were Jeannie and Alex, in their best winter frocks (when had mother and daughter grown to look so alike?) and Darius, tired and thin but seemingly unbruised by his ordeal. *But not Will.* That absence clutched at Sophie's heart.

Alex's attention was all on Darius, her heroic and ill-treated Persian prince. "When they arrested you, Darius," — and she managed not to see her mother's warning glance — "when they put you in prison, were you awfully afraid?"

"It wasn't really prison," Darius said, "just cells below the police station. But yes, I was frightened — quite a lot. Although," — and he gave Alex a comradely smile across the table — "not half as afraid as when we crossed that crumbling cane bridge."

Late in the evening, after Darius had said goodnight and Major Bradley was alone with the family, the major drew Sophie aside.

"Miss Pritchard — Sophie — do you suppose I could have a quiet word with you?

"Of course," said Sophie, and thought, *Oh dear.* When people asked to have a word with you, it was usually quite a number of words, and perhaps not ones you wished to hear.

"Come into the sitting room where it's warmer," said Jeannie, and the three of them settled by the fire with coffee and liqueurs.

"Miss Pritchard," remarked the major, "after your recent adventures, you must find ordinary life a little dull."

"Not at all," said Sophie wondering, a little apprehensively, what was afoot. "I don't believe I could bear any further excitement."

"Young Alex says you are a true heroine, and I must say, I have to agree."

Sophie felt herself blushing. "Hardly a heroine, Major Bradley. You know that in Alex's world, we are all characters in romantic novels."

"Indeed," said the major, smiling. "But Sophie — may I call you Sophie? You must realize, over these past months you've shown quite extraordinary courage. Certainly it was the courage of your conviction that led you to shout a warning about the bomb. And as to physical bravery — Mrs. Grenville-Smith has told me of how you crossed that cane bridge, without a moment's hesitation, at the risk of your own life."

"I wasn't brave," said Sophie. "I was terrified every step of the way."

"Even so — I've also heard about your encounter with the odious Inspector Grey, and how you stood up to his accusations. I call that true courage."

"Major Bradley, it was *not*. It was anger. I was so angry that I forgot everything I'd been taught about politeness, and self-restraint, and never showing one's emotions. I was arrogant and rude and prideful and self-important. I was all the things I hate about the Raj."

Was there the hint of a smile from the major? But his response was serious enough. "My dear Sophie, there are times when anger — especially righteous anger — is a useful weapon. Far better that, than being afraid."

"But," exclaimed Sophie, "I've been angry for so long, there is so much in this world to be angry about." She had not meant to say any of this — the words spilled out, unbidden. "The way the Raj treats the people it rules, this war that carelessly throws away the lives of brave young men. But even before that . . . " There was a thickening in her throat and her eyes had begun to sting.

"Before that?"

"I think . . . I think I've never stopped being angry since the night my parents died."

Major Bradley gave her a keen look. Sophie was aware that Jeannie, too, in her chair by the fire, was listening intently. The major asked, "Angry at what, Sophie? At God? At the whims of fate?"

Sophie fumbled for her handkerchief, and the major offered his. She wiped at the sudden wetness on her cheeks.

"Perhaps," she said. "But I've read what's been written about the ship — I've overheard what people have said. I think it was not God, or fate, that sank *Titanic*. I think it was just carelessness — a series of mistakes, miscalculations, miscommunication. It was carelessness that condemned my mother and father and all those others to death."

"Then Sophie, there's only one way to deal with that kind of anger, and that's to acknowledge it. And then you try to do what you can, however little it may be, to restore order to the world. If I may ask, how old are you now?"

Surprised, she said "I turned eighteen this month."

"And have you given much thought to what the future might hold for you?"

"The future?"

"I mean, of course, the next few years. Before marriage, and a family, and all that.

Needless to say we hope all our young women will contribute to the war effort — but I'll wager you won't be content with knitting socks for soldiers."

Sophie smiled at that, but she was lost for an answer. It seemed that her days, since she came to India, had been so filled with events and misadventures that she had simply lived from one day to the next. What chance had there been to consider the future? In England young women like Diana Grenville-Smith were nursing the wounded; they drove ambulances at home and on the front; they joined the Land Army and worked in munitions factories. Here in Calcutta the memsahibs dutifully knitted socks while their daughters went to regimental balls and dances at the Club.

"Mrs. Grenville-Smith and I have spoken a few times about your situation," the major told Sophie.

My situation? Sophie turned to look at Jeannie, who gave a slight nod of agreement.

"And," continued the major, "we have something for you to consider. But Mrs. Grenville-Smith knows you better than I, and so I think I best let her continue."

FORTY-SIX

JEANNIE SAID, "I'VE NEVER TOLD you, Sophie, why I became a cryptanalyst."

It was one of many things that Jeannie had not revealed about her past. Sophie said, "I thought perhaps it was because you are good at puzzles."

Jeannie laughed. "Yes, I am, rather. But plenty of people are good at puzzles. Major Bradley noticed that I seemed especially good."

"Before the war," explained the major, "we often called on volunteers as cipher-breakers — classical scholars, linguists and so forth — even people who were very good at crossword puzzles. Still do, in fact. And so when I became aware of Mrs. Grenville-Smith's special abilities, it seemed like a jolly good idea to recruit her."

Special abilities? When Alex was kidnapped, when they all were in danger, Sophie had witnessed a terrifying display of Jeannie's power — but what had that to do with puzzle solving?

Seeing Sophie's confusion, Jeannie said, "Every year our enemies develop more devious and complex codes, and logical deduction can only take us so far. Sometimes in the end those codes only yield to a kind of inspired guess."

"Can you . . . ?"

"Make that kind of guess? Sometimes. Not always. It can come like a flash in the dark, out of nowhere. It seems that if you're born with a special talent — a wild talent — you can be sensitive in other ways as well. In the work that I'm doing, it gives me a certain edge."

It was clear to Sophie what she was about to be asked. *But I'm not like Jeannie,* she thought. *I'm not clever enough . I'm not a scholar, I don't know languages. I'm not ready for any of this.* And yet in spite of all the objections that rushed to mind, she felt a flutter of excitement.

Aloud she said, in a small uncertain voice, "But I'm not very good at puzzles."

Major Bradley laughed. "Sophie, we have puzzle-solvers. We need more people who are capable of those wild imaginative leaps. We need the sort of mind . . . "

" . . . that can dream of fantastic monsters," Jeannie finished for him, "and recognize them as construction cranes."

"And I would be a spy?"

"That isn't a word we use," said Jeannie with a smile. "You'd be an intelligence agent. A gatherer of information. Much the kind of thing you've doing these past months. But not high adventure. Just a job, like any other."

"Not quite like any other," Sophie said.

"No, not quite. And Sophie, we both know that the talents you possess far exceed any of mine. We believe," — and she glanced at Major Bradley — "those abilities could have enormous military value. The kind of visionary experiences you've had these past months — those might happen only once or twice in a lifetime. But in the meantime . . . "

"I would solve puzzles."

"Yes. Once you've learned the trade. Alex still believes that when I spend those long hours shut away in my office, I'm writing novels. The truth is much less glamorous. There's not much romance involved in code-breaking, Sophie. There's a lot of training needed; it's hard, demanding work, and only occasionally is it exciting."

"Just so," put in the major cheerfully. "No derring-do. No dashing about with pistols. "Or," he amended, "one sincerely hopes that there is not."

FORTY-SEVEN

*E*VERYTHING IS ARRANGED! WROTE ALEXANDRA. *In July I will be setting out with Yongden for Shigatse in south central Tibet. I have received my invitation from the Panchen Lama, the abbot of Tashilhunpo monastery, who is second only to the Dalai Lama in power and rank. Sir Charles Bell will be furious of course, as will the missionaries in Gangtok, when they learn that I have crossed that border so long closed to them.*

It will not be an easy journey. There are British soldiers stationed along the border with orders to turn travellers back. Nonetheless, I have my invitation. We intend to slip across on horseback, with a pack mule to carry our tents and provisions. I am determined that nothing will be prevent me from achieving my life-long dream of exploring the Forbidden Kingdom.

"Sir Charles will be livid," said Tom. He's already convinced that she is the agent of a foreign power — though he can't be sure which one. In any case, I doubt she'll ever be allowed back into Sikkim."

Then perhaps, thought Sophie, she'll return to Calcutta to collect her books and belongings. It would be splendid to see Alexandra again, and share with her everything that had happened since they parted. She thought with happy recollection of those weeks at the hermitage. Her life might be very different now, if that odd, erudite, passionate little woman had not challenged her to find a pathway out of the shadows.

Meanwhile, Jeannie was sorting through the morning's mail. "My goodness, here's another letter from Sikkim. "

"From Sir Charles? He'll be asking us to dissuade Alexandra from this latest folly."

"No, it's from Lady Bell, that's her handwriting," Jeannie said as she reached for the paper knife. And then, unfolding the letter she gave a small astonished gasp. "Why, it's news of Will!"

Tom's smile abruptly faded. "Bad news . . . ?"

Sophie's throat tightened with dread. She put down the cup she was holding and tea splashed over the cloth.

Jeannie, looking up from the letter, said quickly, "No, no, not a bit of it, it's better than we could have hoped. Sophie, listen to this."

"I am so happy to share with you some excellent news. Sir Charles and I have had word from the authorities in Belgium. It seems that Will Fitzgibbon, who you know was missing in action, has just been located. He is presently in the Abbeville Military Hospital in northern France."

Tom voiced the question that Sophie was too frightened to ask. "Does she say how he is? How badly injured?"

Jeannie shook her head. "Just that he is alive, and if all goes well is expected to recover."

Will is alive. Injured, who knew how badly? Sophie would not allow herself to think of the terrible wounds that soldiers could suffer, and still survive. Will was alive. For now, that was all that mattered.

Forty-Eight

J EANNIE CAME IN CARRYING TWO books and set them down on the table. "When I first decided to study cryptanalysis," she said, "the major told me there were two stories I should read."

Sophie picked up one of the books, expecting it to be a textbook. Instead, she read with surprise the ornate gilt lettering on the dark red cloth: *Tales of Mystery and Imagination*. "I was never allowed to read Edgar Allan Poe," she said. "My mother said he was much too frightening."

"As indeed he is, and that was very wise of your mother," said Jeannie. "But all the same I'd like you read 'The Gold Bug' — as I did, years ago."

The second book was *The Return of Sherlock Holmes*, and there was a bookmark tucked between the pages. Jeannie said, "If you've read H.G. Wells, I'm sure you've read Conan Doyle. But perhaps not this story." Sophie opened the book to the page Jeannie had marked, "The Adventure of the Dancing Men."

"Both tales are based on substitution ciphers," said Jeannie. "They're as good a place as any to begin."

୨ଛ

"In the present case — indeed in all cases of secret writing — the first question regards the language of the cipher; for the principles of solution, so far, especially, as the more simple ciphers are concerned, depend upon and are varied by, the genius of the particular idiom. In general, there is no alternative but experiment (directed by probabilities) of every tongue known to him who attempts the solution, *until the true one be attained.*

Sighing, Sophie marked the page and set aside the book. Poe's convoluted, old-fashioned prose was not easy to follow. Her thoughts returned, with anxiousness, and uncertainty, and amazement, to the strange new fact of her existence: *I am to be a spy.* While she mastered the art of code-breaking, Major Bradley would find her a junior secretarial post in some minor government department. But spying — the stuff of cloak and dagger novels — was the job she would be trained to do.

Could her gently bred mother, who found Poe's tales of fantasy so frightening, ever have imagined her in such a career?

She decided to leave the gold bug for later and turned instead to the livelier adventure of the dancing men.

৪৯

In the morning's mail there was a letter for Jeannie from her daughter. "Diana is well, and keeping her spirits up," Jeannie reported, "though she says the hours are very long, and the Matron is impossible to please . . . Oh, and listen to this, Sophie — she has seen Will Fitzgibbon, and sends news."

I went with my friend David Cameron to visit Will Fitzgibbon at a convalescent hospital in Berkshire. He seemed very pleased to see us, and was in quite good spirits. I gather that physically, he is over the worst, though he may be left with some facial scars.

Jeannie glanced down the page. "Perhaps I should not read this next bit."

"Oh please," said Sophie. "I need to hear it." Whatever the worst was, she told herself, if Will was over it, then the news must be good.

The wounds we worry about most, with these young soldiers, are the ones we can't see. They return from battle with such dreadful damage to mind and spirit. Some young men I have nursed have been rendered mute by their experiences, and some stare blankly at nothing, as though seeing things too horrible to bear. They call it shell shock — though the military does not like that term, and means to forbid its use.

However, Will seems to be doing not too badly, so he may yet make a full recovery, in mind as well as in body. He seems very fond of your Sophie, and I've given him your Calcutta address so that he can write to her.

And after a week's anxious wait, a letter arrived from Will:

Basildon Park, Berkshire

My dear Sophie,
Diana Grenville-Smith very kindly came to visit me and has given me your Calcutta address. As you see, I find myself once again in hospital, though this is an excep-tionally elegant one. Basildon Park is an abandoned eighteenth century Palladian mansion taken over by the army for the care of convalescents. I'm told that I am mending well, and this morning I was fit enough for a turn around the overgrown and long-neglected garden.

I have very little memory of how I came by my injuries. When they found me, they say I was wandering aimlessly through a wooded area somewhere in France. (Where exactly, I am not permitted to say.) It seems I had suffered a severe concussion. There was also the matter of several broken ribs, and some rather nasty damage to one side of my face.

They tell me also that I am suffering from nervous exhaustion. The doctors say that the mind can take longer to recover than the body, but they are confident that this too will pass.

Still, it could take some time, and it would not be fair to ask you to wait. But I think of you every day, Sophie, and would dearly love to see you again. I gather that when I'm well enough to leave here, they're putting me behind a desk in Overseas Supply, so I expect to be in London at least until this war is over.

I'll wait, thought Sophie fiercely. *Of course I'll wait. How could you imagine I would not?*

Somehow, without knowing quite when or how it happened, she had stumbled her way out of the shadows. Given time, she knew that Will could do the same.

She found paper and pen, sat down at her desk, and wrote in a firm round hand: *My dearest Will . . .*

AUTHOR'S NOTE

Sophie, in Shadow continues a narrative which began in *Wild Talent: a Novel of the Supernatural*, set in London and Paris a quarter-century earlier.

Though Sophie, like Jeannie, is a fictional character, her story too plays out against real historical events. The details of the 1915 Christmas Day Plot to seize Calcutta and overthrow British rule in India were not revealed until thirty years later, when a former Viceroy of India mentioned them in his memoirs. That particular plan was discovered in time, and a bloodbath averted. However, as Sophie learns, where there is one conspiracy afoot, there are likely to be others.

Sir Charles Bell's uneasy relationship with Alexandra David Neel, and Alexandra's persistent attempts to cross the border into Tibet, are well documented in Government of India files and in Alexandra's own writings. (Eventually Alexandra did fulfill her dream of travelling in Tibet, to Sir Charles' immense displeasure.)

For background material I am especially indebted to the following titles: *Like Hidden Fire: The Plot to Bring Down the British Empire,* By Peter Hopkirk (Kodansha America); *Women of the Raj,* by Margaret MacMillan (Thames and Hudson); *Calcutta* by Krishna Dutta (Interlink Books); *Calcutta* by Simon and Rupert Winchester (Lonely Planet Books); *Forbidden Journey: The Life of Alexandra David-Neel,* by Barbara and Michael Foster (Harper & Row); and *Two Under the Indian Sun,* Jon and Rumer Godden's delightful memoir of their East Bengal childhood, 1914 – 1919 (Alfred A Knopf).

On a personal note: in 1912 my maternal grandfather, Arthur Pritchard, decided to give up his struggling farm in Worcestershire and emigrate with his wife and five children to Canada. Their plan was to make the crossing on the much-publicized maiden voyage of SS *Titanic*, but they were too late to book accommodation, and travelled instead on the next available ship out of Southampton. In the years leading up to the centennial of the *Titanic* disaster, I was reminded of how such random events can decide the very fact of our existence.

Sophie's story, like all family histories, is a narrative of "What Ifs?"

Acknowledgements

A very special thanks to my indispensable first readers: my husband Pat, my daughter Sue, my friends and fellow fantasists Sandy Hunter and Mary Choo, and members of the Helix speculative writing workshop.

Epigraph: Another World by Pat Barker (London: Penguin Viking 1998, 1999), pages 270-271. Copyright © Pat Barker, 1998. Reproduced by permission of Penguin Books Ltd. and Aitken Alexander Associates.

The quote from H.G. Wells' *The War of the Worlds* is reprinted by permission of United Agents on behalf of: The Literary Executors of the Estate of H.G. Wells.

Sophie, in Shadow is Kernaghan's ninth book in the fantasy genre. Her first young adult fantasy, *Dance of the Snow Dragon*, was set in 18th century Bhutan. It was followed by *The Snow Queen*, which won an Aurora Award for Canadian science fiction and fantasy, and was shortlisted by the Canadian Library Association for Best Children's Book of the Year. *The Alchemist's Daughter*, set in Elizabethan England, was shortlisted for the Sheila Egoff Prize for Children's Literature and the Manitoba Young Readers' Choice Award. *Winter on the Plain of Ghosts*, which also appeared in 2004, is an adult historical fantasy set in the ancient Indus Valley civilization. *Wild Talent: a Novel of the Supernatural*, a novel of spiritualism in Victorian England and fin de siècle Paris, appeared in 2008, and was shortlisted for a Sunburst Award for Canadian Literature of the Fantastic. Eileen Kernaghan lives in New Westminster, British Columbia.